D0866342

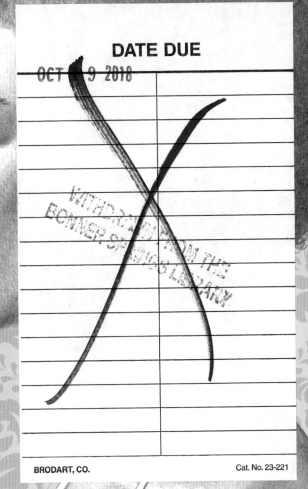

Pride

Also by Ibi Zoboi

American Street

IBI ZOBOI

BALZER + BRAY

An Imprint of HarperCollinsPublishers

Balzer + Bray is an imprint of HarperCollins Publishers.

Pride

ISBN 978-0-06-256404-7 (trade) — ISBN 978-0-06-289112-9 (special edition)
— ISBN 978-0-06-289358-1 (special edition)

Typography by Liz Dresner

18 19 20 21 22   PC/LSCH   10 9 8 7 6 5 4 3 2 1

❖

First Edition

To Joseph, my forever love

ONE

IT'S A TRUTH universally acknowledged that when rich people move into the hood, where it's a little bit broken and a little bit forgotten, the first thing they want to do is clean it up. But it's not just the junky stuff they'll get rid of. People can be thrown away too, like last night's trash left out on sidewalks or pushed to the edge of wherever all broken things go. What those rich people don't always know is that broken and forgotten neighborhoods were first built out of love.

The new owners are moving into the mini-mansion across the street today. For the last few months, construction crews have been giving that abandoned house an Extreme Makeover: Bushwick Edition. They gutted and renovated the best thing on our block—that run-down, weed-infested, boarded-up house. Now it looks like something that belongs in the suburbs, with its wide double doors, sparkling windows, and tiny manicured lawn.

I pull back the curtains to greet my little corner of Bushwick and Jefferson Avenues, my very own way of stretching out my arms and yawning at the morning sun. This is where I see words swim in and around my neighborhood like dust from overhead train tracks. It's all poetry. So I pull those words together and try to make sense of it all: my hood, my Brooklyn, my life, my world, and me in it.

Everything is how it's supposed to be—except for that mini-mansion that's like a newly polished pair of Jordans thrown in with a bunch of well-worn knockoffs.

Still, I remind myself that today is special, and I won't let those new neighbors moving in mess that up. My big sister, Janae, is coming home from her first year of college, after finishing up a school internship, and she'll be spending the rest of her summer break with me. Mama's got a Welcome Back dinner all planned out. I fluff up my thick, kinky fro and throw on an old pair of jean shorts. They're hand-me-downs from Janae, and they're even tighter than they were last summer. Mama has joked that my curves have finally kicked in at seventeen—not that I was waiting for them. The Haitian-Dominican Benitez sisters already get enough attention on the street and at school as it is.

I slept late, but I can hear my younger sisters, Marisol,

Layla, and Kayla, joking and laughing in the kitchen as they help Mama with the Welcome Back dinner—peeling batatas, seasoning the chicken, boiling the habichuelas, and soaking the dry salted fish for bacalao. Papi must be sleeping in because he worked overtime last night, and I know he wants to avoid all that noise. I get it, though.

Sometimes I would rather hear the sound of roaring buses, zooming cars, and blaring music over my sisters' constant cackling—and Mama's too. She's the loudest of them all, and she can be the most embarrassing. Me, Papi, and Janae are the quiet ones in my family. All three of us would rather fold into each other on the couch, reading a book or watching a documentary, than gossip with Mama.

I'm about to head into the kitchen when I see it. Across the street, a blacked-out SUV pulls up in front of the new mini-mansion. They're here! We all took bets on what these fools were going to look like—*black* and rich, or *white* and rich. One thing's for sure: they had to be rich to move into *that* house. The passenger side door opens and—never one to lose a bet—I yell out at the top of my lungs, "The rich people are here!"

In no time, Marisol, who's two years younger, is standing right beside me. Not because she's the fastest, but because she has the most to lose with this bet. Me and my money-hungry sister, aka Money Love Mari, bet a whole twenty dollars that it's a young white family moving in, because that's what's been happening all over Bushwick.

"Come on, white boy, come on," Marisol says while clapping and pushing up her thick glasses. "Let's make this money!"

But a black woman gets out from the passenger side, just as Layla walks in and shouts, "Yes! We won! Give us our money!" She and her twin, Kayla, bet that it would be a rapper or a basketball player and his supermodel wife, and we'd all be famous by association just 'cause we live on the same block.

But then the driver hops out, along with two passengers, and we can't believe our eyes. Stepping out of the back of the car are two of the *finest* boys we've ever seen. Fine, *black* teenage boys. Marisol and I have definitely lost the bet, but no one cares.

The entire family gathers on the sidewalk and looks as if they've stepped into a different country. And as I watch them, I realize there's a difference between expensive-*looking* clothes and actually being expensive. The woman is wearing all white, as if she's going to a fancy boat party, and uses her sunglasses to push back her long, shiny hair. The man has on a sky-blue button-down shirt with rolled-up sleeves, and he keeps his sunglasses on. And then there are those two boys.

"Oh. My. God!" Layla is the first to say anything, as usual. "Who are they?"

"Rappers and ballers! Give us our money, Marisol," Kayla says.

"No they're not! Those boys look like they're from One Direction or something," Layla says. "Look at how they're dressed. I know a baller when I see one. And no rapper will be wearing them kinda shoes."

"They're more like *Wrong* Direction. They don't look like they belong here," I say.

"But they're cute. Are they our age? Let's go say hi." Kayla grabs her twin's hand and rushes out of the bedroom. The twins just graduated from middle school, and ever since they turned thir*teen*, it's been all about *teen* everything—clothes, music, and *teenage* boys. They have way more swag than me, Marisol, and Janae put together, with their matching outfits and hairstyles.

I rush to follow my sisters, but Mama steps out of the kitchen and stops me in my tracks by holding a wooden spoon out in front of me.

"Ey, no you don't," she says with a hand on her hip. Then she turns toward the door. "Kayla and Layla! Get back in here!"

The twins stomp back into the living room.

"But Mama," Marisol says. "The new neighbors are here! And they're *black*!"

Mama brings down the wooden spoon and raises her eyebrows. Her hair is tucked beneath a colorful satin scarf, and her wide gold hoop earrings almost touch her shoulders. She's rocking her signature Brooklyn loves Haiti T-shirt and pink velour sweatpants, even though it'll be hot as hell in that kitchen. A smidgen of bright red lipstick only covers her bottom lip, and the blush on her deep-brown cheeks shows she's making an effort for Papi. I know exactly what she's about to say, so I count down in my head. Five, four, three . . .

"Zuri, you should've been at the Laundromat by now. All the dryers'll be full. Marisol, you sorted the darks already? Layla and Kayla, strip your beds and strip ours too, if your father is up. Zuri, sweep the front stoop and the staircase when you get back. I want it all perfect for Janae," Mama says, in almost one breath. Then she walks right past us and into our bedroom to look out the window.

When Mama kept having baby girls back-to-back, our parents decided to turn the big living room into a bedroom for all five of us. Mama and Papi sleep in the bedroom in the back, near the kitchen and bathroom, and what was supposed to be a dining room is where we all gather on the couch to eat and watch TV.

In less than a minute, Mama returns from our bedroom wearing a big, bright smile. "On second thought, I think y'all should go say hi to our new neighbors! And sweep the front stoop while you're at it."

I let my sisters rush out ahead of me just as Papi shuffles out of the back bedroom.

"Janae's home?" he asks while scratching his pot belly. His thick, curly fro is smashed on one side and one eye is bloodshot. He didn't get enough sleep. He's been working nights at the hospital cafeteria again.

Mama shakes her head. "No, but you can go introduce yourself to those nice folks across the street."

He waves his hand. "I already did. They came to check out the house last week."

"Papi! Why didn't you tell us?" I say.

"What's to tell?" He plops down in his usual spot on the recliner chair and grabs an old Howard Zinn book that he's read a hundred times. Papi reads as if the world is running out of books. Sometimes he's more interested in stories and history than people.

"Zuri! You coming?" Kayla yells from downstairs. The whole block is used to our loud mouths by now, but I wonder what the new neighbors will think when we yell each other's names out from windows, down the block, and even from the corner bodega.

Outside, Marisol and Layla are already across the street, talking with the two boys. Their parents must have gone inside. Kayla grabs my arm, and before I know it, I'm headed across the street too. My little sister is holding my hand like I'm some kid, but by the time we step onto the curb, I pull away from her and cross my arms.

Both of the boys look to be about my age, seventeen or so. They have smooth brown faces that look unreal—the forehead, eyebrows, and cheekbones of models. One of them is a little taller and slimmer than the other, but they definitely look alike. They have to be brothers. The shorter one has a head full of thick hair, and even though he's shorter than his brother, he still towers over my sisters and me. The tall, slim one has a close-cropped fade and a hard jawline that moves from side to side as if he's gnashing his teeth. I try hard not to stare, but it doesn't really matter—my sisters are already holding it down in the thirst department.

"And this is ZZ. Aka Zuri Luz Benitez." Layla pronounces my whole name while pointing at me.

"Hi, it's just Zuri," I say, holding out my hand to the taller boy with the fade. "My friends call me ZZ."

"Darius." He takes my hand but only grabs the tips of my fingers and shakes them softly. I quickly pull away, but he keeps staring down at me out from under his thick eyelashes.

"What?" I say.

"Nothing," this boy named Darius says as he rubs his chin and fidgets with his collar. He's still looking at me.

So I roll my eyes at him. But I can still feel him staring even as I turn my whole body away from him and face his brother.

"I'm Ainsley," the other boy says, giving me a firm shake. "We, uh, just moved in. Obviously!"

"Nice to meet you," I reply, using the good manners that Mama has drilled into us.

"Totally! I can't wait to explore Bushwick. Your sister has been telling us all about it," Ainsley says. He's smiling way too hard. It's the kind of smile that'll get him punched in the face if he bumps into the wrong guys from around the way. But still, he's nice, like a happy puppy in a handmade sweater that the white people in our hood like to walk around, while Darius seems more like a cranky bodega cat. "And please ignore my baby brother, he's just grumpy that we had to leave Manhattan."

"Dude, hey, I am not grumpy. It's just an . . . adjustment," Darius says, crossing his arms.

"What a hard *adjustment* for you," I say, my curiosity about these boys turning off like a switch. I don't appreciate anyone throwing shade at my neighborhood, especially from people who say words like "totally" and "dude." I give Darius my mean Bushwick mug, but it doesn't seem to register. He just stands there with his upper lip curled as if he's smelling his own stank attitude.

"We've been living here our whole lives. So you can ask me anything," Layla continues. "I can show you where the basketball courts are, and introduce you to some of the brothas on the block. You gotta meet Colin. He cool. But Marisol knows where you can get the best prices for bread and milk. Don't go to Hernando's bodega, though. He jacked up the prices ever since he put up that 'organic' sign."

I'm about to stop Layla from embarrassing herself further when Marisol interrupts her first, ready to initiate one of her business transactions.

"I'm Marisol, but you can call me Money Love Mari, for reasons you will soon understand. Can I interest you in any financial advisory services? It doesn't look like y'all need any, but things are a little different out here. You *might* wanna learn how to stretch a million dollars in the hood. I charge by the hour. Small bills, please," she says, revealing her signature braces and pushing up her glasses.

"Stretch a million dollars in the hood? Okay." Ainsley laughs. "Money Love Mari. I like that."

Marisol smiles, looks down, and hugs herself. She didn't see that coming—a compliment, followed by a dimpled, bright smile. She can't even look him in the eye after that.

"Y'all need to come over here and help me!" someone yells from across the street. A yellow cab eases up to our building, and I see Janae poke her head out the back window.

I start to run to her across the street, but a bike bell makes my heart leap out of my chest. I freeze as a bike screeches toward me, and I don't even react when one of the boys pulls me out of the way. The bike races past me with the rider holding up his middle finger as if *I* almost totaled his hipster bike with my five-foot-four-inch frame. I knew these new bike lanes were trouble. No one watches where they're going anymore.

I catch my breath and realize that it's Darius who has a firm grip on my arm as my sisters surround me. The shock wears off, but he's still squeezing my arm a little too tight.

"Uh, you can let go now," I say.

"Right." Darius releases his hand. "You're welcome, by the way."

"Oh, thank you," I mumble, trying to be polite. He steps away from me, and his face is a little more relaxed now, but I can still smell his stank attitude. *Thanks, but no thanks,* I say in my head.

Janae jumps out of the cab, looks both ways on the busy avenue, and rushes over to me.

"Zuri!" she says as she wraps me in a hug. "I know you missed me, but don't go jumping in front of traffic for me!"

"Missed you too, Nae-nae," I say, and give her a squeeze. We both rock from side to side before we let go, but Ainsley has already stolen Janae's attention. Her eyes are glued on him, and I know that in less than a second, she's taken in his whole swag—haircut, face, body, clothes, smile, and even his teeth. I don't blame her.

"And you are?" Janae asks, grinning from ear to ear.

"Ainsley," he says, only smiling back at her. "Ainsley Darcy. We just moved in. And this is my younger brother, Darius."

"Oh, hey," Janae says with her usual sunshine, rainbows, and unicorns. Then there's a long second of awkward silence, except for the usual Bushwick noise. I can tell that Janae is looking for something interesting to say, as if she didn't just come down from upstate after meeting new people and having new experiences and learning new things. My big sister is not good at this whole game, even though she's spent a year away at college.

Ainsley grabs her hand and says, "I'm sorry. You didn't tell me your name."

"That's our big sister, Janae Lise Benitez!" Layla says. "She goes to Syracuse."

"Syracuse?" Ainsley says. "I go to school upstate too. Cornell."

"That's nice," Janae responds, trying really hard to look cool while the twins start giggling.

I'd be lying if I said Janae wasn't like a second mother to me, to us—especially after Mama had the twins and she was busy doing any- and everything for them. Nae-nae never tried to take our mother's place, though. She was simply our big sister—two years older than me, and six years older than the twins. She did our hair, helped pick out our outfits, gave us advice but still let us make decisions for ourselves. She was the sticky sweetness that held us all together.

My sisters bawled their eyes out the day she left for college. I took a long walk from here to the Brooklyn Bridge, because that's how I deal with stuff. Now she's home for the summer, and we are back to being the Fierce and Fabulous Five Benitez Sisters, according to the twins. Or, the All About the Benjamins Benitez Sisters, according to Money Love Mari. Or the Five Heartbeats, according to Janae, because she says we are her heart.

Out of the corner of my eye, I catch Darius shaking his head, as if this whole scene is nonsense. I turn to him and shake my head too, letting him know that we are on the same page, that everybody except him and me is being ridiculous. But he doesn't return the gesture. He looks away. Whatever.

The cab driver honks at us, still waiting for his fare.

"Oh, shoot, I got to go pay for that," Janae says, and starts to head back across the street. My sisters and I follow her.

"Bye, Ainsley! Bye, Darius!" Layla calls out behind us.

"Bye . . . Janae!" Ainsley says, and Janae reaches for my hand and squeezes it as if to say she can't believe any of this— that those boys look *good, and* they're going to be living across the street, *and* the one named Ainsley was seriously checking for her.

It's not until I reach our stoop that I look back to see if Darius smiled, or waved, or watched me cross the street, or if he stayed as stiff and cold as a tree in winter. But he's already gone inside the house.

TWO

SOMETHING ABOUT THE Darcys moving in makes me want to hold Bushwick a little bit tighter and for a little bit longer, as if it's slowly slipping away—like Janae, and high school, and me being small enough to curl into Papi's arm while he reads the *New York Times*. The streets are fully alive as a hot summer night sets in, loud with the sounds of the wheels on a shopping cart rolling across jagged sidewalks, the J train passing by on the aboveground tracks on Broadway, and hip-hop and reggaeton dancing out of someone's opened window.

Our apartment is busy with Mama finishing up Janae's Welcome Back dinner.

Mama treats our special family dinners as if they're a block party—she invites the whole building, and sometimes even all of Jefferson and Bushwick Avenues too. So if my sisters and I don't grab our plates before Madrina and her nephew, Colin, come up for their share, there won't be any left. Even though the dinner is for Janae, it's possible she could miss out on the food too.

That's just how Mama is—she's the heart of the neighborhood, pumping stewed chicken, banan pezé, sancocho, bacalao, pastelitos, and black rice to just about every single household on our block. And in exchange, she gets all the gossip.

Madrina, the owner of our building, who lets us rent for mad cheap, has to catch her breath when she reaches our apartment. She celebrated her sixty-fifth birthday last year and rarely makes it up because of her bum knee and her weak heart. She's wearing her signature white dress and white head wrap. She's always draped in all white because according to her, she has to be a walking and talking crystal ball for all the fortune-telling she does (although she hates it when we call it fortune-telling). "Es para los espíritus," she says—so the orishas can *see* her when she asks them for favors.

Her colorful beaded elekes hang long and low from her neck, and they sway from side to side like a pendulum when she walks. Madrina claims that she was a beauty queen back in her day in San Juan. That's how she got crowned as a Santería priestess of the goddess Ochún. She embraces all that is love and beauty. So she walks around with a full face of makeup. Her powdered foundation is always two shades too light, her blue eyeshadow

15

is applied so thick that it's almost navy, her eyebrows are a thin drawn-in line, and some of her red lipstick is on her teeth.

"Oh, mija! Look at you, college girl!" Madrina bellows when she sees Janae. Madrina's thick arms almost wrap around Janae twice. She limps over to the couch where Marisol, the twins, and I are huddled together, eating from our plates. We all get up to make room for her as she slowly eases down near the armrest. We take spots on the carpeted floor, and when Madrina's finally settled, it feels as if the whole apartment has let out a deep, long sigh.

The warm, smoky smells in the apartment are a big, wide hug. Mama's high-pitched laughs and Madrina's booming words are music—accordions and congas in a merengue or compas band. When she sings her orisha praise songs during her ceremonies down in the basement, I can feel it all the way up here on the third floor. And when Papi looks up from his food to add his two cents to the conversation, it's like his words are a tambora adding deep wisdom to all that superficial gossip. My sisters' giggles are güiras, and together, it's a party, even without actual music.

Even though I'm planning to leave home for college, I know all that music will still be here, waiting for me, when I get back.

"Beni!" Madrina calls out to Papi. "Did you see the blessings that Ochún has brought to your door? Dios mío! Your prayers have been answered!"

"What are you talking about, Madrina?" Papi grunts. He's

in his usual spot on the recliner in a corner of the room where he can be away from it all but still keep a close eye. His cup of black Bustelo coffee sits on a nearby stack of books, and he's inhaling a plate of arroz con habichuelas. We all know that Papi doesn't like to be interrupted when he eats. But Madrina doesn't care.

"Your rich son-in-laws just moved in across the street. Their father is an *investor*. Ochún has delivered your daughters' husbands nice and early so you have a few years to get to know them. You should invite them over."

We're all as quiet as a steaming pot of rice as we wait to see Papi's reaction to hearing the word "husbands."

Then Madrina lets out her usual deep, booming laugh, and the whole apartment seems to shake. She laughs so hard that no other sound comes out of her wide mouth. Her face is wound up into a knot and a tear rolls down her cheek. "Look at your father's face, girls! He don't want you to date. He wants you all to stay right under him until each one of you is old and gray like me."

"Not if I have anything to do with it," Mama says. She always tries to one-up Madrina by shouting even louder. But she doesn't have the same depth in her voice, so she's just loud. "I won't mind at all if my daughters are playas. Have fun, date around, see what's out there. Don't tie yourselves down like I did. Those boys are cute, aren't they, Janae? Which one you like? I like the one with the afro for you. I saw him waving."

Papi shakes his head at Mama. "I'm outta here," he mumbles, getting up from his recliner and taking his plate with him.

Janae and I exchange looks, because we already have our lives figured out and they don't involve these new boys across the street. After college, she's getting a teaching job and her own apartment in Bushwick. And I'm going to Howard University and will live on campus in my own dorm room where I can stretch out my arms and legs and not have to hit a little sister in the head while doing so. After I graduate, I'll get a job and my own apartment here too. None of those scenarios involve a boyfriend or a husband. So I say, "I have no interest in either of those boys, Madrina. I'm going to college and getting a job—I don't need an *investor* to take care of me."

Papi comes out of the kitchen where he was getting started on the dishes, comes over to me, and gives me one of his awkward fist bumps. "Now that's my baby girl! She got her own mind."

"So who are those two boys for, Madrina? Me and Kayla?" Layla asks. Of course she does. Layla is the boy craziest one out of all of us. "Ey, slow down, Speedy Benitez!" Madrina says. "You get in line behind Marisol. And then the baby, Kayla, is right after you."

"So I'm not gonna get married until Marisol gets married?" Layla whines. "Do you see her, Madrina? I'll be waiting *forever*!"

"Yes, you will. And there are two ways to examine the

institution of marriage," Marisol begins, and the whole room sighs because she's about to spill out a series of facts, numbers, and statistics that all have to do with the thing she loves most in the world: money. "It can mean either that marriage is the false notion that love is forever and a woman is left to depend on her husband for financial support, or that two incomes are better than one. Love is abstract. Money is not."

"Hah! Now *she's* the one who'll marry for money," Madrina says. "Put all your eggs in *that* basket, Beni."

"Aw, come on!" Janae finally says, and everybody gets quiet. "This is the *future*, Madrina. We're thinking about our careers and goals and breaking barriers. And yes, Marisol, we're thinking about making money!"

"Career before family? Como una gringa?"

"No, Madrina," I say. "Not like a white girl! Like . . . a woman! Any woman."

"Como Beyoncé y Jennifer Lopez," Janae adds.

"My baby," Mama says, smiling and cocking her head to the side. "She spends one year at college and she thinks she knows everything."

Janae's face drops, and I can tell that stung her a bit. My big sister is carrying the whole intellectual weight of the family now that she's the first one to go to a four-year college.

Mama had Janae while she was a teenager herself and only went for a couple of semesters before dropping out when she got pregnant with me. Papi did two years at a community college and is proud of his associate's degree. They got married at a very, very young age. And thank los espíritus, as Madrina would say, that they at least liked each other. They more than liked each other, though. They are actually still in love.

I know this because as we're all yapping in the living room, Papi washes the dishes, cleans the kitchen, and comes back to offer Mama a glass of water while he takes her empty plate. Some of the other men on the block—Bobbito, Wayne, and Hernando—have always teased him for being such a lover boy. I've seen him do little things like this all my life. And I know in my heart of hearts that their kind of love is very rare.

While Madrina and Mama are still running their mouths, I nod at Janae. She gets up to wash her dish, and when she's done, she slips out the door. I keep my eye on the twins because they'll be the first to notice. But they're on their phones now, probably going through their endless streams of selfies. I wait a couple of minutes before I tiptoe across the small living room and quietly shut the door behind me.

Janae is in the hallway waiting for me. We grin at each other.

"Well, hello, ladies," someone says from the second floor, and we both jump.

We look down over the banister to see Colin's big ol' head coming up the last flight of stairs. Janae and I sigh and roll our eyes at the same time.

"And may I add, you look hella fine, Janae," Colin says when he gets to our door.

"Oh, shut up, Colin," I say.

But he ignores me and goes straight for my sister. He takes her hand and kisses it, pretending to be a gentleman and not the thirsty player that he is.

We've known Colin all our lives because he's Madrina's nephew. And since Madrina doesn't have any children, she sort of adopted Colin as her own—she's even said that Colin is going to inherit the building. Every summer he'd spend weeks with her, with us. When we were little, Colin was like the big brother we never had. He turned the rope for us when we needed an even game of double Dutch, he pretended to be whatever we wanted him to be—a monster, a chupacabra, a Death Eater—so he could chase us around Maria Hernandez Park. But three summers ago, he turned eighteen, moved in with Madrina, and started acting funny around us—with an almost full beard, and a much deeper voice. He stopped playing games with us, and one day he approached Janae with a letter professing his undying love for her. Since then, it's never been the same.

"Welcome back, Janae," he says, all smooth and looking up at her with puppy-dog eyes.

Janae pulls her hand away and shakes her head. "Hurry up before the food's all gone."

When he opens the apartment door, the first thing Madrina says is, "Colin, mi sobrino! Did you see your competition that just moved in across the street?"

The door slams shut behind him, and finally Janae and I have a quiet moment to laugh at all the ridiculousness that is our home, our family, our lives.

THREE

A NARROW DOOR at the end of the hallway opens up to a ladder that leads to the roof. This is our happy place, way above it all. It's also our secret place, because Papi forbids us to go up there for obvious reasons: we might fall to our deaths. So even though he padlocked that door a few years ago, we managed to find a way to unlock it and escape out onto the clouds.

If Madrina's basement is where the tamboras, los espíritus, and old ancestral memories live, then the roof is where wind chimes, dreams, and possibilities float with the stars, where Janae and I share our secrets and plan to travel all over the world, Haiti and the Dominican Republic being our first stop.

Janae always has a pin in her hair, and it only takes her a

second to crack open the lock. We climb the ladder, open the door, and step out into the warm early evening air.

Late June in Brooklyn is like the very beginning of a party—when the music is really good, but you know that it's about to get way better, so you just do a little two-step before the real turn-up starts. It's still light outside at eight o'clock in the evening, and from up here on the roof, we can watch the comings and goings of everybody on Bushwick and Jefferson Avenues.

And just like from our bedroom window, we can't avoid the fancy mini-mansion across the street. All my life, I've stared at a gaping hole in the roof, the boarded-up windows, the slow, creeping forest that was starting to suffocate that house. Once, my sisters and I took bets that a tree would grow right in the middle of the floor and it would keep growing and take the house with it. And then we could claim it as our very own tree house—our home in the sky.

But no. It's a mini-mansion now. The gaping hole is fixed, the forest around it has been cut down into a perfect patch of too-green-for-the-hood lawn, and the new windows are so tall and wide that we can see right into the top and bottom floors of the house, with its shiny hardwood floors, white walls, floor-to-ceiling bookshelves, art that looks like it was made by a kindergartener, and furniture that looks like it belongs in a doctor's office.

For weeks, there were so many people coming in and out of that house painting, moving furniture, and decorating that we thought it was going to be a museum or, as Janae suggested when I texted her a picture, a bed-and-breakfast.

"I can't believe they had other people decorate their house," I say while stepping closer to the edge of the roof. "Like, they have enough money to pay someone else's salary for something they could've done themselves."

Janae gently pulls me away from the edge. "I'm just wondering why they'd want to move here. I mean, they could've done that upstate or something. When I take the bus up to school, you should see all these big houses on top of hills, Z."

"Really? Did you meet any friends who live in those houses? Were they . . . *black*?" I ask sarcastically.

"You do know there are black people who have money out there in the world, Z, right?"

"Of course there are. But why come into the hood? I thought everybody was trying to kick us *out*."

Janae stands beside me. Our shoulders touch, so I put my arm around her and pull her in. She puts her arm around my waist and leans her head on my shoulder. "Maybe we can ask them," she says, almost whispering.

"Ask who?"

"Ainsley and Darius. They look good, Z."

"I don't think so, Nae," I say. "They live too close. It'll be awkward."

Just as I say this, we spot Ainsley in one of the windows. He's running his fingers through his thick fro, which, even I have to admit, makes him look really, really good. Janae and I glance at each other, and she smirks. Ainsley doesn't look up. But we step back so he can't see us, anyway.

There's a wide blue tarp hidden beneath an old wooden slat on the roof. Janae and I pull it out and lay it across the sun-warmed tar, away from the edge of the building where only two feet of brick and concrete keep us from open sky. I sit cross-legged on the tarp while Janae pulls her knees up to her chest.

"How come rich people don't like curtains?" I ask no one in particular.

"They're showing off," Janae says, lifting her head from my shoulder.

"You think they're *that* rich?"

"No. They probably got a good deal on that house."

"They definitely got a good deal on that house. So they're just hood rich."

"They're more than just hood rich, Z. But anyway, Ainsley was nice," Janae says as she spreads her legs out in front of her.

"Janae . . . ," I warn. "Sistas before mistas!" I ease closer to her and put my head on her shoulder now. After a long minute of taking in the warm air and sounds on our block, I ask, "Does it feel good to finally be home?"

"Yeah, but I can't wait to go back," she says.

I pull my head up from off her shoulder and stare at her. "What? You just got here."

"I know, but Z, I need the space. I need the wide-open space to stretch out my arms. I need the quiet to hear myself think."

"Oh no, Janae! Mama was right. One year at college, and you decide you don't wanna be in the hood no more?"

She pauses and takes in the dead-serious look on my face before responding in her sweet, calm voice. "Honestly, I don't. I'm applying for some study-abroad programs. I wanna travel, Z. I wanna see the world. *Then* I can come back."

I never knew that's what she wanted. I can hardly imagine it—my sister on the other side of the world? What if she decides to never come back? "Aw, come on, Nae. You've been outta the state. Let's see," I say, counting on my fingers. "That time with Mama when we went to the mall in New Jersey, the water park in Pennsylvania . . ." I keep two fingers up, thinking of anywhere else we've been and if they count as a whole other state.

"Don't think too hard, Z, 'cause that's it. We've been to a mall and a water park out of state. That doesn't count for anything."

"Dang," I say, and let my shoulders drop because she's right. Only once have Mama and Papi taken a bus up to Syracuse for a weekend. It would've cost too much for my sisters and me to go, so we stayed behind, and they sent us videos and pictures of the bus ride through woods and small towns and places nothing like Bushwick or Brooklyn. "Read to travel," Papi always says.

Every book is a different hood, a different country, a different world. Reading is how I visit places and people and ideas. And when something rings true or if I still have a question, I outline it with a bright yellow highlighter so that it's lit up in my mind, like a lightbulb or a torch leading the way to somewhere new. It's usually enough to make me forget I've barely left Bushwick.

"Okay, Z," she says. "Enough with the pity party. Senior year's coming up. What's the master plan? 'Cause you gotta get out of that apartment."

"Gotta get out of that apartment," I repeat. "Wow. I can't believe by this time next year, I'll be leaving for college. Marisol and the twins are gonna lose their minds 'cause there'll be two less bodies up in that house!"

"That's what I said about *you* before I left."

"But I didn't lose my mind. I missed you, Nae-nae."

"No, no, no. You're not allowed to miss me. You gotta get your mind right from now, Z. Study for your next SATs, get your college list ready, financial-aid packages, scholarships . . ."

"I know, I know," I say.

"Seriously, Z. If you don't do these things, you won't ever get outta there. Home will always be here, and Bushwick will always be Bushwick."

"Will it, though?"

She's quiet for a moment and looks out over the other houses and buildings. "Okay, well, what if you come back home and get started on your career, and then you could actually buy something in Bushwick and afford Hernando's bodega prices no matter how many 'organic' signs he puts up."

I laugh, and then remember what I'm supposed to be working on this summer. "You think this will make a good topic for my essay to get into Howard?" I ask. "How to save the hood?"

"It depends on how you frame it. What's your angle, your thesis statement? What are you trying to say?"

I pause for a moment, thinking about my hood and how even though families grew up and changed, things essentially stayed the same, until now.

I uncross my legs, and at the same moment, the door to the mini-mansion opens and out come the Darcys. Each of them has changed into something different. The mother is now wearing a flowery sundress and the father is in a pink button-down with khaki slacks. Ainsley is dressed in a crisp T-shirt and jeans. Darius is dressed exactly like his father.

"Hi, Darius! Hi, Ainsley!" We hear someone yell out from below. It's Layla, of course, yelling out the window.

The two boys look up. Only Ainsley smiles and waves back. Then he looks up even farther and sees Janae. She freezes, and I can tell that she doesn't know whether to wave or scoot back so he doesn't see her. Then she relaxes and stares until Ainsley disappears into the back seat of the SUV, along with Darius, who never once even looked up.

The Darcys drive away and turn down Bushwick Avenue. I wonder where they're going. They just walked into that fancy house—why would they leave it so soon, even if it's for a few minutes? I wonder if they've been out of the state, out of the country. I wonder about all the places and things and new experiences their money has been able to buy them.

So I start to ask Janae, thinking that she might have the answers, but her eyes are fixed on the setting sun, and I'm sure her dreams are floating with the clouds.

I can see the dim moon in the distance, the orange-blue sky, and can hear the bustling sounds of Bushwick as they wrap around us, and this roof becomes like a cupped hand holding the two of us up.

"Z?" Janae says without looking at me.

"Yeah?"

"Do you think I have a chance?"

"With who?" I ask.

"Ainsley," she says, her voice soft.

"Shit" is all I say.

FOUR

IT'S THE FIRST Saturday morning of summer vacation, and the apartment is a delicate bubble—quiet, full, and round with me and all four of my sisters squeezed into one room. We're all about the same size and height now, still sleeping in the beds we've had since we were little.

Two bunk beds are pushed against the walls in our bedroom, and Janae's single bed is right beneath the front window.

I'm up before my sisters and in the middle of my book, a highlighter and pencil in hand, just like Papi taught me. I'm reading *Between the World and Me* and thinking about Ta-Nehisi Coates's mecca, Howard University, and how it'll be like a whole other country with no outsiders moving in to change things up and throw things away; where the faces of the people are the same now as they were back in 1867, when Howard was first founded; where even though people come from different parts of the country and the world, they speak the same language—and that's black, and African, and Caribbean, and Afro-Latinx, all the things that make up me: Haitian, Dominican, and all black.

I finish the chapter I'm on and peek out the window—checking to see if anyone is setting up for the block party yet. But all I see are the Darcy boys in front of their house. Ainsley is jumping about, punching the air as if he's ready to fight. Darius is stretching out his legs, and both of them have patches of sweat around the necklines of their T-shirts. Something about the way they're dressed lets me know that they definitely weren't playing ball at the park, nor were they doing pull-ups on the monkey bars like all the other guys in the hood.

On the corner, a white woman is scooping up her dog's poop with her plastic bag-covered hand. She pulls off the bag, ties it up, and tosses it into a nearby bin, then pets her dog as if he's done a good job. I spot Mr. Turner from down the block, standing outside Hernando's with his cup of coffee. Soon he'll pull out the plastic crates, turn them over on their sides, and wait for Señor Feliciano, Stoney, Ascencio, Mr. Wright, and some of the other grandpas to join him in a daily game of dominos or cards while smack-talking about politics and the latest soccer match.

When the street lights come on, they'll move out of the

way for the younger guys—Colin and his crew, who just stand there checking out girls, drinking not-juice from bottles, and also smack-talking about politics and the latest basketball game. Then the block party and the music will move in, and everyone will eat and dance late into the night. It's one of my favorite days of the year. And it's like a smaller version of my other favorite days: going to the Dominican Day parade with Papi and the Puerto Rican Day parade with Madrina, and repping the Haitian flag at the West Indian Day parade with Mama. Our block parties bring everybody in our hood together, though—the Dominicans, Haitians, Jamaicans, Puerto Ricans, Mexicans, Panamanians, African Americans, and white couples too, who are buying up a lot of the brownstones down the block.

My neighborhood is made of love, but it's money and buildings and food and jobs that keep it alive—and even I have to admit that the new people moving in, with their extra money and dreams, can sometimes make things better. We'll have to figure out a way to make both sides of Bushwick work.

That gives me an idea. I grab my small laptop and type the first words of my college application essay to Howard.

Sometimes love is not enough to keep a community together. There needs to be something more tangible, like fair housing, opportunities, and access to resources.

My younger sister, who is a self-proclaimed finance

whiz, says it best: Love is abstract. Money is not.

I type, delete, type, and delete over and over again. I inhale. Close my eyes. And let my fingers dance across the keyboard.

How to Save the Hood

If my name was Robin
I'd steal the tight corners
Where hope meets certainty
To form perfectly chiseled bricks
Stacked high to make walls
Surrounding my Bushwick

Sometimes I don't go to the other side
Where Bed-Stuy or Fort Greene
Are guarded and armed with coffee mugs
And poodles on leashes

I don't see any more homeless pets
Like the ones that used to gather
In the junkyard on Wyckoff Avenue
Beneath the overhead train tracks
Like marks on the arms of junkies
Who used to stumble down Knickerbocker

Boxing the air, fighting the wind
Suckerpunching a time
When those graffiti-covered walls
Used to be background canvases
For old ladies in house slippers
Pushing squeaky shopping carts
Around those tight corners
Where hope meets certainty

Hope is wishing that corners will
Turn into long, unending streets
Where all the traffic lights turn green

Certainty is knowing that corners
Will always be home
Where ninety-degree angles
Are the constant shapes in our lives

Always a sharp turn

By late afternoon, our apartment is a smoky sauna of Mama's cooking for the block party. I've gotten used to the smells by now, and so has our block, and maybe our whole neighborhood too.

All the windows are wide open to let out the smoke, and my

sisters and I have stripped down to just shorts, tank tops, and aprons, along with hairnets and gloves when we're handling the food.

The new people moving into our neighborhood probably think that our part of Bushwick can't get any louder than on a random Saturday night in July.

The bass has been pumping since noon, and with that kind of noise, there's no reading, thinking, or dreamily staring out the window for me. The deejay is set up right in front of our stoop, and our whole building seems to dance to the rhythm of the music. None of us can sit still. Even as I help cook, I bop, snap, do a little two-step, and follow along as Layla and Kayla practice their dance moves for the block party's talent show.

The block party is something we've been putting together for the last couple of years, ever since Mama became the one-woman planning committee of the block association. She manages to bring together the ladies on Jefferson and Bushwick to cook and set up a few tables at the other end of the block, while Papi and his homies set up grills on the side-walk and large coolers of beer near our stoop. People from other blocks sit on lawn chairs all up and down the sidewalk. Kids run and ride their scooters. On each end of the block, two or three cars block off traffic. This is Mama's dinners on steroids.

Finally we're done cooking and everything is ready to go into aluminum containers. We help carry the food downstairs and then are free to go enjoy the party. Janae goes to fix her makeup before coming to join me on the stoop. She holds a plastic cup of ice cream and sits next to me while bopping her head to the deejay's latest beat. Behind the deejay is a ministage where the talent show contestants will perform—right in front of the Darcy house. This was never a big deal before, since it used to be abandoned.

"You think they're pissed?" Janae asks as she scoops up a spoonful of ice cream.

"Who?" I ask, playing dumb.

"You know who I'm talking about. The Darcys. They're not even here a week and already our block is bringing all this noise to their doorstep."

"I don't care," I say.

"Yes, you do."

"No. I do not."

"You should've seen your face when Darius saved you from that bike."

"I don't care what I looked like, Janae!"

She just laughs at me, and I give in and laugh too. No one can stay mad at Janae for long.

I spot Charlise making her way over to us from Bushwick Avenue. And as if she already knows I'm looking straight at her, our eyes meet. She smiles her Charlise smile—a head nod and one corner of her mouth turned up.

I hadn't texted her that the new neighbors had shown up,

because I wanted her to see them for herself.

"Z-Money. What up?" she says when she reaches our stoop, giving me one of her hard daps with her man hands. Charlise is a baller who's been accepted to Duke on a basketball scholarship. She's a year older than me, and between her and Janae, I know all about what to expect for applying to college. But Charlise is planning on coming back after Duke too.

I shimmy my shoulders, clap one time, do a little two-step with my feet while still sitting on the stoop, a little dance move with my hands, and Charlise figures it out real quick.

She gasps, nudges Janae so she can sit in between us, faces me, and asks with wide eyes, "What happened, Z? Is this an inside story, or an outside story? Hot tea or iced tea? Spill it! I got my teacup right here!" She pretends to sip from a tiny cup while holding out her pinkie.

Both Janae and I start laughing. Charlise loves neighborhood gossip just like Mama.

I fix my mouth to start telling the story of how those Darcy boys moved into the hood when the music changes and some of the kids rush to the deejay to do the latest dance moves.

"Aw, yeah! That's my joint right there!" Charlise sings, and takes my hand to pull me up, and that's when I see the Darcys coming out of their house. I automatically stop dancing and sit back down.

"What happened?" Janae asks, finishing her ice cream.

"Nothing," I say, only bopping to the beat a little.

But Janae knows me too well, so she stands up and sees what I just saw. And of course, she waves. "They're coming over here."

"I'm out." I start to stand to go back upstairs, but Janae stops me.

"Aw, come on! What's wrong with you, Zuri? We can't avoid them for the rest of our lives."

"Rest of our lives? Who says we'll know them for the rest of our lives?"

"What are y'all talking about?" Charlise asks. She's still dancing and hasn't noticed the boys.

Janae taps her shoulder and points toward the Darcys with her chin.

"Oh. Hello!" Charlise says. "Who are *they*?"

"Those're the boys who moved into that house," Janae says.

"What? For real, for real?" Charlise says, smiling and wide-eyed.

"For real," both Janae and I say together.

"Damn. They're hella fine."

Janae throws me a told-you-so look.

"I'm not blind, Janae. I know they look good. It's just that they're off-limits," I say.

"Zuri doesn't like them just 'cause they live across the street," Janae tells Charlise.

"I feel you, Z," says Charlise. "The way y'all do things on this block, it'll be like they're your cousins."

"Thank you!" I say. "But, wait. No. I mean, it'll be complicated. They won't be like our cousins. I mean, look at that house."

"Okay. They'll be like your *rich* cousins," Charlise says. "But they won't be *my* cousins. Introduce me, Zuri."

"No!" I almost yell. "Not you too!"

"Look," Janae says. "If those Darcys did all that stuff to that house, then they're gonna be here for a very, very long time too. We might as well get to know them."

"They're not really trying to get to know us, Nae. Yeah, they fixed up that house, and soon they'll want to fix up our whole block. I don't think they're feeling this block party."

"Oh, yeah? Look," she says, pointing with her chin.

Ainsley has joined the group of kids dancing with the deejay. He's wearing a big ol' smile.

Janae starts dancing along. "Hey! Hey! Hey! Hey!" she sings to the music, acting just as corny as Ainsley.

Charlise doesn't join them, thank goodness. She just watches Ainsley and giggles.

Ainsley turns to us, still dancing, and somehow, he and Janae manage to dance with each other while he's a few feet away and she's still on the stoop. Ainsley calls her over. Janae shakes her head and calls him over instead. He and my sister are acting like complete cornballs.

"No, Janae. *Please don't*," I mutter under my breath.

But Ainsley doesn't move, and in no time, Layla makes her

way over to him and starts dancing.

"Uh-uh. No she didn't!" Janae says.

"Your little sister don't waste no time," says Charlise.

The music changes to something different, with a faster beat, and instead of stepping away from Ainsley, Layla grabs Kayla and they surround him.

"Oh, no," I say. "Where is Papi when we need him?"

"They're just having fun," Charlise says.

Ainsley goes along with the whole thing as if he's been accosted by thirteen-year-olds before. He knows all the dance moves, even though he's a little off beat, and this makes him look kind of cute. I'm mad at myself for even thinking that.

I spot Darius watching them too. He's not bopping his head, smiling, or even looking at all the kids around him. He just stands there on the sidewalk, with his arms crossed, acting like he's too good for all this.

"That's the younger brother, over there in the white shirt. Darius," I say to Charlise. "I can't stand him."

"Didn't he *just* move here?" she says.

"Yeah, but look at him!"

"I see what you mean. He has no swag whatsoever. Neither of them do. But at least that Ainsley is *trying*. Come on! Introduce me!"

Then, suddenly, Layla walks over and starts dancing with Darius. I can see from all the way over here that his nose is flared, his lips are turned up, and his brows are furrowed, as if my little sister disgusts him. Layla doesn't notice a thing.

"Do you see his face, Charlise? That whole family might as well be white." I start to get up from the stoop.

"Z! Leave them alone. They're just having fun!"

I ignore Charlise and quickly walk down the stoop, stomp through the crowd of dancing kids, and head straight for Layla. I yank her arm and pull her aside.

"What the hell is wrong with you, Zuri?" Layla shouts.

"I'm sorry," I say to Darius, before turning to my sister. "You need to slow down. He don't want you all up on him like that."

"We're just dancing," she says, rubbing her arm.

"No, *you're* just dancing, while he's over here looking at you like you're a pile of crap."

"Excuse me?" Darius says, eyebrows raised.

"You're excused," I say, side-eyeing him.

In a huff, Layla pulls away from me and heads back to her friends. But I'm not done with this boy, so I give him a death stare. Darius cocks his head back and looks at me as if I'm the one who did something wrong.

"I'm sorry. Who do you think you're talking to?" he asks.

"I'm talking to you, Darius Darcy! I saw how you were looking at my sister."

"She came up to me." His voice is deeper than I remember, and he has a little bit of an accent I can't place. It's definitely not Bushwickese or anything close to a Brooklyn twang. "And don't talk to me that way. I'm not one of your *boys* from the hood."

I throw my hands up and look every which way to see if anyone else is hearing this.

"Oh, trust me." I laugh. "I know for damn sure you're not one of my *boys*. And it doesn't matter if she's my sister or not. You've met her! If you would've *looked* at us, you would've known that. But I guess money doesn't buy manners, right?"

He doesn't have an answer for that question, of course. His jawline moves from side to side, and he looks over me, around me, and maybe even through me. Finally he says, "Well, I know when I'm not welcome," and then he turns and walks back into his mini-mansion.

I stare at Darius's back, my fingernails digging into my palms. I take a deep breath to release negative energy, like Madrina taught me to do. "Be like the river and go with the flow," she says. The block party is only getting started, and I can't let Darius Darcy and his stank attitude kill my vibe. I breathe out.

While I wasn't looking, Janae went over to dance with Ainsley. She's in a dreamy haze as he pulls her close. It's all so corny, and Janae is falling for it. I cross my arms and narrow my eyes.

If Janae is the sticky sweetness keeping us sisters together, then I'm the hard candy shell, the protector. If anyone wants to get to the Benitez sisters, they'll have to crack open my heart first.

FIVE

I'M SITTING ON the front stoop, and the words to this college application essay aren't coming at all, or maybe they're floating around my head and I just need to look up and grab each one.

Change. Money. College. Job. Space. Family. Home.

If I listen closely enough, I can hear Bushwick's volume turning down real slowly. Getting quiet. My sisters don't believe me when I tell them that even though it's still noisy, our neighborhood is getting quieter and quieter every summer, as if the tiny musical sounds that fill up my hood are popping like bubbles, one by one, and disappearing into empty silence. Anybody who's been in Bushwick long enough is like a musician, and when they leave, we lose a sound.

Nothing pours out of me. Nothing escapes through my fingers. I sigh and slam my laptop shut just as the front door squeaks open and out comes Janae, wearing strappy sandals and newly shaven, oiled legs. I don't even have to look at her face to know that she's got on her signature summer-shimmery-glow makeup and lip gloss.

"What you all dressed up for?" I ask.

"I'm not dressed up," she says, playing dumb.

I only glance over at her to know that I was right. Janae doesn't have anything planned for the rest of the summer—no job, no internship, so her butt isn't going anywhere on a Monday afternoon in July. But her phone keeps buzzing, and she's texting as if the world is about to end. Janae doesn't have a lot of friends, either. Or rather, the two who she has are not in this neighborhood anymore, and her college friends are off traveling for the summer.

She glances across the street, and I let out a long, deep sigh.

"What?" she asks.

"You tell me what."

"Fine. He invited me over."

I clutch my laptop and stare at those wide double doors. I hate those doors. "Janae, I haven't seen you in months. Can we do something? Take the bus downtown? The movies? The bookstore? Anything?"

"Yeah, of course. We got the whole summer, Z," she says,

45

smiling and staring at the house across the street.

"You're going over there now?"

"Uh, yeah." She gets up and smooths down the back of her sundress. "I wanna see what it looks like on the inside. To think, they turned that place around in, what, a few months?"

"Almost a year. I saw the whole thing. Every single day. I can imagine what it looks like on the inside. I'll just draw you a picture if you want."

She ignores me and steps down from the stoop.

"Papi's not gonna like this, Nae," I say as a last resort to keep her from ruining her life. My life. Our lives. Our family gets along with every single person on this block, which makes block parties run smoothly; which makes walking home when it's dark real safe; which makes walking to the bodega in a night scarf and pajama pants not a big deal. The Darcys moving in changes all that.

"I need to see some design ideas for when I buy my own run-down house in Bushwick and renovate it," she says in a dreamy, la-la-land voice.

"That's not gonna happen, Janae, because people like them don't wanna be around people like us," I say out loud. "Especially Darius."

"Zuri, you're being ridiculous" she says, and sashays her round behind and short summer dress across the street.

"It's about to rain, Janae!" I shout behind her.

46

"Good!" Janae says, without looking back.

I try to turn my attention to my essay. I try to not care. I force myself to write, and like always, broken words spill out. A rough, jagged poem, like the steps on this stoop, like the sidewalk in front of this building. Like everything around me right now.

Love is like my sister, Janae. She is springtime tulips
and pastel colors. She is sun rays beaming
through windows where dust particles dance and kiss
in the light. She is tender kissing scenes on TV,
and then afterward practicing on soft pillows
at night. She is the warm space between Mama and Papi
while they sleep and the bills are paid and the fridge is full.
She is made of honey and sugar and summer fruits
oozing gooey sweetness and catching
bees and flies. Buzzing. Annoying. Like the ones
in that house across the street.

Dark clouds over Bushwick have a kind of magic to the them. At least that's what Madrina says. Clouds are never just clouds in my hood. So when the sun takes cover and the thunder rolls, I know something's about to go down.

It starts drizzling, and in seconds, it pours. The house across the street tugs at me. Maybe my sister is wishing that I was with her to see the stainless steel appliances and the doctor's office furniture. Or maybe she can't stand being in there another second and she doesn't want to be rude, so my coming over will be her saving grace.

My laptop is getting wet, so I tuck it beneath my shirt, as soon as I step out onto the sidewalk.

Neighbors are running toward their buildings, and puddles are starting to pool along the edges of the sidewalk. I don't bother covering my head. By the time I reach the house's gate, my hair is wet, limp, and heavy against my forehead and cheeks.

Those doors are even nicer up close, but I still can't stand them because they're like gates to a whole other world. There isn't a doorbell, but there's an intercom with a small screen. I press the button, and a warped black-and-white version of myself appears on the screen. I turn and look to see where the camera is located, but it's well hidden. Of course these people would have a security camera at their front door, and probably an expensive alarm system too. Not even Hernando has his bodega on lockdown like this.

The door swings open and I freeze where I'm standing, wet and cold, with the cool laptop pressed against the bare skin underneath my shirt. It's Darius who's opened the door. I don't dare look at his face. I look past him and into that sterile house.

"I came for my sister," I say.

"Good. You can have her," Darius says.

This time, I definitely have to look him dead in the eye. "Seriously?"

"Yes. Seriously," he says, looking back at me.

He opens the door even wider, but I don't come in. He just stands there looking at me until, finally, he extends his hand as if reluctantly welcoming me to his humble abode.

I step right into that squeaky-clean living room with my wet sneakers. I can feel his eyes on me, and when I glance over, he's staring down at the floor. Rainwater is dripping from my clothes and onto the shiny wood. I don't care. I'm sure they're paying somebody to mop it up.

"Where is she?" I ask.

"Where do you think?" he says with a half smile.

"Janae!" I call out nice and loud, and my voice echoes throughout the whole house. The ceilings in the living room are high, there's a staircase leading up to even nicer rooms, I'm sure, and at the far end of the floor is the kitchen, with tall and wide windows facing what used to be a weed-infested forest. Fancy gold and bronze designs line the edges of the walls and ceilings, and this mini-mansion looks like it was built for princes and princesses. "Janae!" I call out again.

"Do you really have to yell out like that?" Darius says, and walks over to a small box against a wall in the living room and presses a button. "Ainsley. Her sister's here."

"'Her sister's here?'" I repeat. "I do have a name, you know. And so does *my sister*."

"Zuri," he says, nodding at me. "And Janae." He extends his arm toward the stairs as if to say "after you." But he doesn't actually say a word.

"Oh, you've been paying attention," I say, flashing a fake smile.

I pull the laptop from beneath my shirt, and he quickly takes it from me, setting it down on a small empty table near the stairs. I make a mental note to not forget it when I leave. I didn't plan on going this deep inside their house.

When we reach the top of the stairs, I hear voices, giggling and talking. I hear Janae. But my eyes are surveying every single corner of this house. There are no dust bunnies, no clutter, no papers, clothes, or junk. Nothing, as if no one lives here. It's a straight-up museum.

"Where's all your stuff?" I ask as Darius leads me down a long hallway lined with closed doors.

"Stuff? We don't have stuff. We have the things we need," he says.

"You need all this space?"

"Space is much more valuable than . . . *stuff.*"

"Well, what's the point of having all this space if you don't have stuff to fill it with?"

He stops, turns to me, and cocks his head to side. "Have you ever been in a completely empty room, just sitting there to let your thoughts wander?"

I cock my head to the side too, and think of something

smart to say, or to ask. Anything besides a simple no, which would be an honest answer, but he doesn't deserve an honest answer from me. "What's the point of doing that?" I ask instead. And as soon as the words fall out of my mouth, I want to scoop them back up and stuff them back in.

He sighs, rolls his eyes, and keeps walking down the hall.

He doesn't get to do that. He doesn't get to think that my question is a stupid one. He doesn't get to ask me about sitting in an empty room when that's probably what I want most in this world right now—an empty room without sisters and parents and stuff.

"That was a real dumb question, you know," I say, trying to take back that moment because I have to have the last word.

But he doesn't answer me, and we reach a wide-open room filled with L-shaped couches and giant pillows. I should've noticed the people first, but a huge flat-screen TV catches my eye. It takes up a whole wall. This room might as well be a straight-up movie theater, as big as that screen is. Ainsley is playing some video game, and the volume is turned down. There's soft music I don't recognize playing in the background, above us, below us. I can't tell, because the smooth sound seems to come from everywhere. Then I spot Janae in a corner of the couch with her sandals off, her feet curled under her, and looking way too comfortable.

I pop my eyes out at her to let her know that this whole situation is not okay, but she's smiling from here to Syracuse.

She's way too happy to be up in this house with some rich boy she just met. Janae is past thirsty at this point, she's the Sahara Desert.

"Hi, you must be . . ."

I almost jump out of my skin because the girl seems to come from out of nowhere. I'm so fixated on Janae and that TV and the couch and that music and the room that I don't even notice a light-skinned, straight-haired girl getting all up in my face to hold out her hand.

I only take the tips of her fingers. "Zuri," I say, still distracted.

"Carrie. I go to school with Darius," she says.

I glance at Darius without even looking at this girl Carrie, and I immediately know that this little exchange is code for "Don't take my boyfriend."

I want to tell her that nobody's checking for her bougie man; instead I just reply, "Oh, that must be so nice for you."

"You've come to hang out? Maybe you can get the boys to stop playing these stupid video games," Carrie says. She plops down on the couch, opposite Janae. Carrie is kind of pretty in a typical magazine supermodel way; the type of girl these Darcy brothers would like. But my sister got her beat in the curves department. Still, Janae is not supposed to be here on a double date.

"Yeah. About that. Um . . . Janae?" I say, cocking my head to the side, winking, furrowing my brows, anything to let her know without my having to say a word that she has to get the hell up out of here.

"Take a seat, Zuri," Ainsley says. He's now sitting on the leather chair with one leg over his knee as if he's the grown-up chaperoning this whole thing.

Out of the corner of my eye, I see Darius walking to the other end of the room, and that's when I spot the pool table in front of a giant floor-to-ceiling bookshelf. A grand piano is pushed to the corner, and I can't believe how much I couldn't tell from the outside how enormous this house is.

"Or do you want a tour, uh, Zuri?" someone asks. It's Carrie again.

"You live here?" are the first words to come out of my mouth. Clearly she doesn't, but it's as if she's the queen of this place.

She chuckles. "No, but I've already gotten a tour. I can show you around if you want. You've never been in a house this big before?"

I must've blinked a hundred times in one second before landing my eyes on this Carrie. She saw it all over my face and tried to take back what she said.

"I mean, who lives in houses anymore? It's Brooklyn . . . ," she says. "You're, like, in an apartment, right?"

I just stare at her for a long second before saying, "Yeah. And you're right. I've never been in a house this big before, and I think it's a waste of space. You can fit five families up in here and solve Bushwick's housing problem in one shot. But . . . like your boy Darius said earlier, y'all don't have *stuff*, y'all have things you *need* like pool tables, baby grand pianos, and giant flat-screen TVs."

Carrie looks over at Darius, who is smirking, rubbing his chin, and staring at me.

"Touché, Ms. Benitez," Darius says. "See? I remembered your whole name."

Now it's my turn to smile. "I'm not impressed, Darius Darcy. And I'm *definitely* not trying to impress you." I cross my arms and put my neck and whole body into those words so they can sting him. Then I turn to my sister. "Janae, you ready?"

Now *she's* popping her eyes out at me. She uncurls her legs from beneath her, and Ainsley turns to give her a pleading look. Janae only smiles as she gets up.

"I need help with my essay," I say, to get her off the hook. I don't want those boys thinking she's rude, because she's far from it. I'll take the blame for messing up whatever she and Ainsley got going right now, as long as I can stop it.

"I got you, sis," Janae says.

Ainsley gets up from his chair too. "I'll walk you two ladies out." He wraps an arm around Janae's waist, and she leans into him.

"What are you working on?" Darius falls in line behind me as we walk down the long hallway.

"You heard me. An essay." I ignore him and follow Ainsley and Janae.

"You're going to summer school?" Carrie asks. I guess she followed us too.

Clearly they all want me to stay and chat. But I don't even give her the benefit of an answer to that dumb question.

"Sorry about her," Darius whispers behind me before we walk down the stairs.

"No need to apologize for your girl," I say without looking back. But I can feel that he's just a step behind me.

Darius doesn't say anything, which lets me know that this Carrie really is his girlfriend. It's not until we're back down on the first floor heading toward the front door that I look at Darius. Our eyes meet. I quickly turn away.

As Janae walks out, I catch Ainsley gently taking her hand, then letting it go. Janae smiles, and this whole moment settles in my belly like a piece of boiled batata. I can't let her come here again. I can't let this seed of a thing between those two take root, sprout, and become some sort of full-blown love affair. If I do, I'll lose my sister for the whole summer.

Ainsley says something to me along the lines of goodbye and come again, but I ignore him and brush right past him.

We're not even on our front stoop when Janae says to me with a giant smile, "He's taking me out this weekend!"

No, he is not! I think, and roll my eyes hard at my big sister.

SIX

"I SAW YOU!" Madrina sings as she sits on her leather armchair and wipes down her unlit seven-day candles with a Florida-water-dampened white cloth. The whole basement smells like that sweet cologne. If the roof of my building is where Janae and I steal quiet moments, then the basement is where I dive deep into my own thoughts and dreams with Madrina and her claims of comunicando con los antepasados. To Madrina, and all her clients, the basement is home to Ochún, the orisha of love and all things beautiful. For them, this is a place of magic, love, and miracles.

These spirits and unseen things, as Madrina calls them, don't make sense to me. Of course they don't. I can't *see* them. But it's Madrina's wisdom that unties the tight knots of my life, so I play along with what she does for a living and try to believe in these spirits.

"You were running across the street in the rain to those boys' house." Madrina says this as if she's a tattle-telling five-year-old, but I know she's just messing with me.

"I was going to get Janae," I say, pacing around the basement. After Janae told me she was going out with Ainsley this weekend, I came straight down here for Madrina's advice.

The smoke from Madrina's cigars, sage, and candles forms iridescent clouds all around the room. The tables are covered in statues of saints, colorful candles, black dolls in fancy dresses, crystal bowls of candy, bottles of perfume, and the shimmery gold and yellow colors that flavor the whole place. When it's fully decorated, the basement looks like a giant birthday cake for some pretty girl's quinceañera. Madrina laughs. No matter how big or small the joke or not-joke, she laughs that same hearty laugh. "So both of you were in that house? Bueno. You two don't waste no time."

"Madrina! It's not like that. I'm trying to keep Janae *away* from that house. From Ainsley."

"What's the big deal, mija? She likes a boy. That's it. She's a big girl, you know."

I shake my head. "They're arrogant. That's what's the big deal. You should see their house, Madrina."

I stand in front of a small table covered in only yellow and gold things. Yellow is Ochún's color. I remember asking

57

Madrina when she was trying to teach me this tradition why the color of love isn't pink, or red. Think of the golden sun, she said. It makes everything on earth fall in love—how the ocean kisses land, how land nestles trees, how swaying trees always whisper sweet nothings into our ears.

"So which one is Ainsley? The cute one, or the cute one?" She laughs and I shake my head.

I sigh big and loud. "Those boys don't belong here. And they changed everything about this block by renovating that house. Papi says the property values will go up, and the taxes too. Is that true, Madrina? You'll have to pay more taxes because of that nice house?"

"Zuri, mi amor! Don't you worry your little head about taxes and property values. You're seventeen. That's not your job. Your job is to fall in love!"

"I didn't come here for love advice!" I say.

"Yes, you did. You want to know that your beloved sister is not falling for a playa." She winks at me, letting me know that she's using slang correctly.

"I already know everything I need to know, Madrina." I unfold my arms and take a seat on the empty chair near her small table.

Madrina has a crystal ball on that table, as well as tarot cards, small bones from god knows what, coins from god knows where, shells, stones, pieces of folded paper, and a small collection of cigars. But that's all for show. Most times, she just sits there pulling from a plain ol' cigarette and talking to her clients about any- and everything. She'll drop hints here and there about who has a crush on them, who they should marry, who they should divorce, or if there's a side chick or side family in the picture. And she's always on point. She says that the spirits guide her thoughts, but I think she just has good intuition.

Madrina takes out a lighter from her bra. She lights a stick of incense and puts it between her teeth. The smoke dances across her face, then travels up around her head as if it's saying a prayer over her thoughts and memories.

I'm seated directly across from her, and the Nag Champa scent tickles my nose, but I don't tell her this. "Okay, fine," I start. "This is what's gonna happen: Janae is gonna go out with that guy. They're gonna spend all summer together and Janae's never gonna spend a minute with me, and—"

Madrina puts her hand up to stop me from finishing my list of future complaints.

"I keep hearing Janae's name. Why you so worried about your big sister? It's her life."

I exhale and let myself sink into the chair a little bit. Madrina has disarmed me. "I don't want Janae to change," I say real quiet.

Madrina closes her eyes and starts humming. She extends her wide, cool hands over the table. I take them. She rubs my hands. She holds them for a long minute. Then she opens her eyes and grins. Her face is smooth for her age, but the wrinkles on her neck are like ripples in the ocean; the tiny brown spots above the neckline of her white dress are like small, muted suns.

"No, mija. *You're* gonna change."

"Me?" I tense up. "But Janae . . ."

She squeezes my hands and I relax again. I close my eyes. She inhales deep, and she begins.

"Listen, Zuri Luz. Let your big sister be. Let things change."

"Maybe," I reply. But my heart isn't ready to let my big sister drift away.

That night, our doorbell buzzes. Well, not our doorbell, but the one downstairs, because ours broke years ago. The downstairs bell buzzes loud enough for us to hear. We're always having visitors who want either Papi or Mama for a game of dominos or to return Tupperware.

"Zuri!" Mama calls out nice and loud from the downstairs. According to Janae, it's the third time she's called my name, and I'm already deep in my book by the time I hear her.

She calls me again. "Zuri! Come down here! You have a visitor."

My stomach sinks, and I hear all my sisters' footsteps rush to either the front window or the door to our apartment. I hear the twins and Marisol shushing each other. I don't get visitors, and Charlise always texts or calls before she comes over. And plus she'd just come upstairs. Mama never calls me down

60

because I have a visitor. So by the time I get to the bottom of the first flight of stairs, I know who it is.

Mama is smiling way too hard. And she winks at me before going back to the apartment. I don't even look at Darius as he's standing there in the doorway. I look at his sneakers and bare ankles.

With my eyes still cast down, he hands something to me. It's my laptop.

"Oh, shit," I say, and grab it from him. I didn't even realize I had left it at his house.

"You're welcome," he says.

"Thank you." I clutch my laptop to my chest.

My chin tilts up, and our eyes meet. I realize how close we're standing. The street outside goes quiet, as if the neighborhood is holding its breath.

He just stands there, and I don't know if he expects me to say something else, or if he's waiting for me to invite him in. I search his eyes for some sort of clue, but he looks sideways, and I don't know what else to do, so I just step back and close the door in his face.

SEVEN

WE'RE ALMOST AT the park when I hear Janae say, "A couple blocks down Knickerbocker was where Carmine Galante was murdered." It's the only bit of Bushwick history she shares with the Darcy brothers during our whole walk to the park. She insisted that I tag along with her and Ainsley on their date, but I had no idea what I was in for—or that Darius was coming too.

When he stepped out of his mini-mansion behind Ainsley, he said he wanted "a tour of the hood."

But I am not a tour guide. And I'm especially not *his* tour guide.

Janae and Ainsley are being all cutesy as they walk, mostly talking about nonsense like the best campus frat parties and their white schoolmates who wear shorts and hoodies in the dead of winter. "Z, who was he again?" she calls out. I'm about ten steps ahead of her.

"A Bonanno crime family boss," I say. Janae was never into Papi's stories about old Bushwick. I was the one who took notes and wrote poems about them.

"A what?" Darius says. He's only a few steps behind me.

"The Italian mob. They ran this whole area way back in the day—drugs, gambling, blackmailing . . . you name it."

"Cool. Sounds like you know your shit."

"I do," I say, and keep walking.

Both Ainsley and Darius look around as if they've never seen buildings like these before—lined up next to each other with colorful signs and words like taquería, botánica, and Iglesia Pentecostal. Once we cross Myrtle Avenue, Bushwick starts to not look like Bushwick anymore.

Darius takes pics of the graffiti-covered walls that are more like art for tourists than for kids who want to rep their hood or show off their skills to other crews.

When we reach the park, Janae hands me a blanket from her bag. Then she and Ainsley go off on their own, leaving me to babysit Darius because he looks like a fish out of water. Or maybe I'm the fish out of water, because no one told me that we were going to some sort of art and music festival for white people.

I look around to see that almost everyone is sitting on

blankets, something we never did when I used to come here years ago. Nobody was having picnics in this park back in the day. We sat on benches and kept our eyes wide open in case anything went down. And something used to always go down. Still, I'm tired of standing, so I spread the blanket out on the dry grass, confident that with all these white people here now, they've cleaned up the rat poop and broken glass.

"Maria Hernandez Park should probably be called *Mary Hernan* Park now instead," I say to Darius as he sits next to me with his hands in his too-tight khaki shorts pockets.

"What exactly are you saying? Why would the name of this park have to change?" Darius asks, raising an eyebrow.

A white woman gets up from her blanket and starts dancing for no reason at all. The music hasn't even come on yet. So it's not really dancing, it's just random gyrating of her hips. "All these white people don't even know who Maria Hernandez was," I reply. "There's nothing 'Maria' or 'ez' about this park anymore."

"Lemme guess. You knew her. Are you related or something?"

I turn my whole body toward him, and he shifts to look at me. "When he was little, my father played with her kids here. She was murdered right inside her apartment for trying to stop drug dealers from selling in this very park."

"Oh," he says. "That's cool."

"That's cool?" I say.

He shrugs, his button-down shirt going tight across his shoulders.

"What's so *cool* about that? How 'bout you say, 'That's fucked up.'"

He leans back on the blanket, away from me, and props himself up on his elbows. "Okay. That's *fucked* up," he says. "And it's *cool* that this park is named after her. And no, it shouldn't be changed to *Mary Hernan* just because white people are here. That doesn't make any sense."

"Of course that doesn't make any sense. It was sarcasm," I say, side-eying him. "If you knew this park like I do, none of this makes any sense."

"I know what sarcasm is." He pauses and stretches out his legs. I have to move back to make room for him. "What's your deal, Zuri Benitez?"

"What's my deal? My deal is that you're taking up this whole blanket. My deal is that I've been coming here my whole life. And I know guys who come out here to play ball and chill, and they look exactly like you." I rub the back of my hand so he knows what I'm talking about. "My deal is that they don't talk or dress like you. And they definitely don't live in a house like yours. So what's *your* deal, Darius Darcy?"

He quickly folds his legs and scoots back, shaking his head and laughing. "Point taken, Miss Benitez."

A loud screeching sound comes from the stage and makes

me jump. A thin white boy with long hair grabs a microphone and shouts, "What's up, Bushwick!"

Everybody around cheers, and it's all so incredibly surreal. "I can't believe this," I say out loud, and grab my phone to take a picture to send to Charlise.

Out of the corner of my eye, I see Darius taking a picture too.

"That's your homeboy?" I ask. "Oh, I'm sorry. I mean, your *buddy*? Your *pal*?"

His nostrils flare, he licks his lips, and he exhales. "That's Jaime Grisham of Bushwick Riot. They're my sister's favorite band. I'm sending her a pic."

He says this as if it's information I should know already.

"Your sister?" I ask.

He nods. "Younger sister."

I take a good look at this band called Bushwick Riot. There's the skinny white boy with the hair, another one wearing a black ski hat, a shorter, chunkier black one with a thick beard, and two girls—a thick white one with bleached hair, and the other is a black girl with mohawk braids. Each one is either behind a keyboard, a drum set, an electric guitar, or a microphone. "Interesting," I say out loud. "Is your sister still in . . . wherever y'all just came from?"

"Georgia's interning in D.C. for the summer."

"Interning?" I nod my head several times because this is all coming together. "Makes sense."

"What do you mean by that?"

I shrug, not really wanting to spell it out for him. "Rock band, interning, tight shorts. Makes sense."

He laughs with his mouth closed. "Your sister doesn't seem to mind."

"My sister's just making new friends, that's all."

"Clearly."

The band starts with a thunderous drumroll. Some people start to move closer to the stage. "So you're a fan of this band too? Bushwick Riot?"

"No. That's Georgia's thing." He inhales deeply, puts his phone into the back pocket of his too-tight shorts, and crosses his arms.

"Is this . . . your thing? Art festivals in parks? Like, how come you don't go to the park to play ball or something?"

He smirks. "You don't leave that little corner of your neighborhood too often, do you?"

I lean back to get a good look at him. He stares at me, but he blinks first. "Just so you know, in this hood, you're just like everybody else. The cops and all these white people will take one good look at you and think you're from Hope Gardens Projects no matter how many tight khaki shorts or grandpa shoes you wear."

I tilt my head to the side, and we stare each other down.

His jaw shifts again, his nose flares. I'm beginning to realize that this is what happens to his face when he's pissed.

"Damn. I thought we were having a nice conversation, but you just went left."

"To the left, to the left," I say, reciting the Beyoncé lyrics while pointing my thumb and tossing my head to the left.

Darius throws both his hands up and shakes his head.

Over his shoulder, I can see Janae and Ainsley on their way back to us. They're both holding little paper containers of food, hardly enough to fill my belly after that twenty-block stroll down Knickerbocker Avenue. They're purposely bumping arms as they walk, and Janae is smiling with her whole body, it seems.

Janae hands me my little paper bowl filled with two small tacos and laughs at something Ainsley says. For the first time since she's come home from college, I can't stand her. She practically begged me to come with her. But now *I* feel like the third wheel, even though there's four of us.

"Actually, Janae, I'm gonna head home," I say. Darius gives me a look as I stand up.

"Wait, why? We just got here," Janae says.

"Hey, man! Yo, Ainsley." A black guy waves at our blanket. He walks up to Ainsley and gives him a pound. Ainsley awkwardly shakes his hand, of course, while this new boy gives him a straight dap like a normal black dude. Darius acknowledges this new boy with just a head nod.

"This is Janae," Ainsley says to the boy, "and this is Zuri."

The new guy nods in Janae's direction, then looks at me and says, "What up, Zuri? I'm Warren."

I pause from picking up my purse and give this Warren a second look. There's a little bass in his voice, a little hood, a little swag, not like these Darcy boys.

He catches me staring at him, but I don't look away. I want him to know that I'm checking him out, and I want Darius to know too. Our eyes lock for a long minute, and it's as if everything around us—that band, those voices, that warm summer breeze, sirens, and honking cars in the distance—all come to a full stop.

"Zuri was just leaving," Darius says, rudely. But Warren and I keep staring at each other.

This isn't the love at first sight Madrina likes to talk about, but it's a you-look-so-damn-good-that-my-eyes-are-eating-your-face thing we've got going.

Warren steps closer to me while pulling out his phone from his back pocket. "I wanna call you," he says. "I wouldn't mind getting to know one of the Benitez sisters too, right, Ains?" He throws a head nod over at Ainsley.

"How you know our name?" I ask.

"I'm from around here, and every dude from Cypress Hills to the Marcy Projects knows about the Benitez sisters with the fat asses."

"Excuse you?" I quickly say. "Don't be talking about our asses!"

"Oh! Pardon me, but you know how brothas get down. And none of y'all were checking for dudes from Hope Gardens."

Now both Janae and I are thoroughly confused. "You're from the projects?" I ask with a screw face.

"You don't have to say it like that, though."

"Hold up. I just mentioned Hope Gardens to this dude over here," I say, pointing at Darius with my chin. "And he didn't say anything about knowing anybody from Bushwick, especially the projects."

Warren laughs. "Darius and I go to the same school, and we're two out of nine black guys in our whole grade. That's about it."

"What school is that?" I ask.

"The Easton School in Manhattan," Janae answers for me, with her eyebrows raised as if this is something impressive. I've never heard of it.

"I got into one of those programs that takes smart kids from the hood and puts them into private schools," Warren says, rubbing his chin. *He* says this as if it's something impressive.

"Private school?" I say. I can't hide the smile on my face, because I am definitely impressed with this boy. He smiles too. Warren's smile is golden. Warren is smooth and easy. Warren is Bushwick.

My phone number just rolls out of my mouth. I don't blink, I don't think about it, I simply throw each number at him as if they're dollar bills and he's a male stripper at a club like in those music videos the twins like to watch.

Out of the corner of my eye, I see Janae trying to hold in

a laugh. Behind her is Darius and his tight jaw. I want him to see what's going down; I want him to see how it's done. This is swag. This is how you step to a girl from Bushwick—a Bushwick *native*.

"Zuri, weren't you just leaving?" Darius asks.

"Nah, I'll stick around," I say. "Actually, Warren, do you want to get closer to the stage?"

"Let's do it," he says, and knocks my shoulder with his.

"Shoot your shot, sis!" Janae says, smiling at me.

Warren stands next to me the whole time Bushwick Riot plays. All around us are the white people doing their strange dances to this punk music, the Whole Foods bags, the colorful blankets, and the kids from around the way who try to carry on as if nothing is changing. But like Madrina said, everything is changing. Old and new are mixing together like oil and water, and I'm stuck here in the middle of it all.

EIGHT

Boys in the Hood

Ball don't lie, how it bounces off concrete
With swag, sway, and dip
The way the girls on the sidelines flip
As you run, jump, shuffle your feet
Your dance moves, like sugar so sweet
From here to the moon, boy, take me on this trip
If I snatch this ball from you, will you kiss me on the lip
Your wink, your smile, your touch like a treat
You hold this ball in your hand like it's your world
You run this block, this hood, my heart

And if I wanna be your girl
I'll steal this ball from you, bounce and spin in a whirl
It's been in my court from the start
I run this whole game, make you fall deep,
   make your head swirl

"Why can't you just rap like everybody else?" Charlise says while balancing my small laptop in her wide hand as she reads my poem. "You got some skills, Z, but if you rapped, you would've *been* had your mixtape by now. And you know Marisol would've *been* selling them on every corner from here to Washington Heights."

We're on a bench near the gate at the basketball courts in the P.S. 151 school yard. Two groups of guys are playing, and Charlise is waiting for a hoop to free up so we can shoot some ball. The school yard has been more packed than usual with guys from around the way. Word on the street is that cops were starting to mess with people over at Maria Hernandez Park. So guys stopped going over there and started coming out here to get some peace. That's something the Darcy boys wouldn't know anything about.

Charlise doesn't really like balling with me, but it's much better than just sitting around chatting and chirping like two birds, she says. She doesn't want us looking like basketball groupies 'cause she's a baller herself. I don't tell her that I'm an undercover groupie because I love watching the boys in my hood play ball.

"You want me to be a rapper while you're a baller so we could be a dynamic duo stereotype?" I say, taking my laptop from her and putting it back into my bag.

"Okay, here we go. Why it gotta be a stereotype, though?" She grabs her ball from beneath the bench and starts passing it between her hands.

"Layla and Kayla still swear that the Darcy parents are ballers and rappers. Well, just the dad . . . the mom is probably just a trophy wife."

"And they'd move to Bushwick, of all places?"

"That's what I'm saying. They're too stuck-up."

"You'd be stuck-up too, Z, if your pops was making bank."

"No, I wouldn't! I wouldn't think I was better than everybody else. I wouldn't look down on other people who look like me. Take Warren, for instance. . . ."

"Warren from Palmetto?"

"Uh-huh. Look at this." I show her his texts in my phone. Since we last saw each other, I've already followed Warren on the Gram and Snapchat. And we've been texting each other about stuff, like how we almost went to the same elementary school. Nothing too deep, so nothing to gossip about with Charlise. "You would never think that he was smart and went to some private school in Manhattan," I say.

Charlise laughs, scrolling through his Instagram and tagged photos. "You don't know the Warren I know. I remember his little scrawny self in the sixth grade right before he got into that program—class clown, always fighting, but yeah, smart as hell. Teachers said he was bored so they had him take this test, he aced it, then they put him in a white school. After that, we never really saw him around the way anymore."

"So he's different," I say, with a half smile. "I thought he was hood. . . ."

"Ay yo, Zuri!" one of the guys from the courts calls out.

I turn to see who it is, and Charlise steals the ball from me. "What up, Colin!" I shout, then wave back to all the other guys who wave at me.

"Colin likes you, you know," Charlise says. "He's *hood*."

"Come on, Charlise," I say. "You know what I meant by that. They could be from around here, but they gotta have something going on for themselves. They gotta have goals and aspirations."

"What if my boy Darius checked all those boxes, *and* has bank? While Warren will still be trying to get his moms, aunties, and grandmother out the projects when he starts making money. There'll be none for you," she says, passing the ball to me.

I bounce the ball, spin, pass it between my legs, and toss it back to her. "Aw, come on! Not you too! I'm not tryin' to get with some dude just so I could get in his pockets! And I can't stand him." As soon as I say this, my phone buzzes in my back pocket. It's a text from Warren.

Let me take you out tonight.

Now I know what it feels like to smile with my whole body, like Janae does, because Charlise asks if it's Warren without even seeing the look on my face.

"You're finally starting to get a little action, Z? It's about time," Charlise says for all the guys to hear. She bounces the ball over to Colin and the group of guys at the nearby basket.

"What's up with me and you, Z?" one of the guys calls out.

"I got a boyfriend," I say. It's not true. But it's not a lie, either. I reply to Warren:

No. Let ME take you out tonight.

NINE

I'VE NEVER REALLY had a reason to keep a secret from my little sisters. But even if I tried, they'd sniff it off me, because it's so tight in our bedroom that there isn't enough space for hidden crushes, unspoken names of boyfriends, and secret dates.

If my phone buzzes with a new text, Kayla will feel it in her top bunk on the other side of our room. If I'm daydreaming about kissing, Layla will see the dreamy look on my face and ask for a name and a physical description. In no time, both the twins will try to find him on social media and stalk him—even if I've made up a name and he's an imaginary boyfriend.

They've already done that with the Darcy boys, because Ainsley is all Janae can think, dream, and talk about. Darius gets it the worst because he's *available*, according to the twins.

But they couldn't find him on social media. I checked myself. The twins double-checked and are still trying to find out if he has an avatar with a different name. Though they did find that girl Carrie, and several pictures of Darius on her page—the back of his head, one side of his face, even his lips. She and Darius definitely have something going on. But then again, she has pictures of other boys on her page too, including Warren.

"I'm going to the movies with Charlise," I say when the twins ask me why I have on lip gloss, my favorite earrings, and extra-tight jeans.

They let it slide, because going out with Charlise means making an effort to look extra cute because we always meet guys wherever we go.

"Just make sure that they have little brothers or cousins for us," Layla says as she stares into her phone. I always ignore her when she says this.

In the living room, Mama and Papi are laid out on the couch watching TV. Mama has her feet across Papi's lap, and he's giving her a foot massage while she talks back to the characters on her favorite show. Without even looking in my direction, Mama calls out, "Ten o'clock! Text or call if you're gonna be late!"

I give them each a kiss on the cheek, and in that moment, I feel like I can fly around the world and back if I want to, because this is what will always be here waiting for me: my parents' love; my loud sisters; my crowded and cluttered apartment; and the lingering scent of home-cooked meals.

And someone different and new, but who still feels like home, is waiting for me outside—a boy from my hood. Bushwick Warren.

I told him to meet me on the corner of Jefferson and Broadway, and he immediately knew that I was trying to keep this little hookup a secret from my sisters—and my parents. He knows where I live and could ring the buzzer if he wanted to. But he's there at the corner waiting with a bright smile.

"You look good," Warren says as he stares at my braids and giant gold earrings. "You're ZZ, all right."

"What do you mean by that?" I ask with a big smile on my face, because he looks extra good with a new pair of fresh sneakers, a crisp tee, and jeans fitted just right.

"I like your style, that's all," he says, extending his arm out to me.

"It's not for you, trust me," I say, taking his arm even though I really don't have to, but it's just there and it's smooth and strong.

"Why can't you take a compliment?"

"'Cause this is not a date." I don't move away or tense up, because even though I don't know him like that, Warren feels like all the other guys from my high school or around the way. I never really had a boyfriend, just guys I messed around with— holding hands while walking down the hall at school, play fighting in the park, a one-on-one game of basketball where he smacks my booty and I smack his face for stepping out of line. We'd go out with a group of friends, and if we were ever left alone, it still wouldn't be a date.

"What is this, then?" Warren asks.

A cab is waiting at the curb, and he opens the door for me. "We're just chillin'," I say as I slide into the back seat.

I pretend that this is no big deal, that guys always pick me up in a cab and open the door for me all the time. "I don't chill," Warren says as he slides in next to me. "I don't really have time to chill. So as far as I'm concerned, this is a date." Then he says to the driver, "Downtown. Court and Montague."

"Downtown?" I ask. "You got that kinda cash?"

He only side-eyes me and I wish I could take it back, but this is Bushwick Warren and no matter how fancy his school is, he's still from HG Projects. So I push further. "Warren? Why don't we just take the bus?"

"Because this is a date," he says, licking his lips.

I laugh. "This is not a date. And look, I don't know who you've been dealing with over there at the school in Manhattan, but like you said, I'm ZZ and you don't have to impress me with no fifty-dollar cab ride."

"I don't have to, but I want to."

"I'd rather you spend that money on food, or a good movie."

"We can do that too."

I just stare at the side of his face as he looks out through the windshield, still smiling. "Are you slingin' dope, Warren?"

"What?" His voice cracks, and he turns to me wide-eyed and with his mouth open. "I already gotta deal with this in school, and now that I'm finally getting with one of the Benitez sisters, I have to answer this question with you too."

"I gotta ask. Come on, Warren. You know ain't no dude from Bushwick will spend their money on a long-ass cab ride just to impress some girl. So you're gonna drop like two hundred dollars on this not-date?"

"Number one: you're not just *some girl*. Number two: I'm not just some dude from Bushwick. I thought I made that crystal clear. And number three: I work for my bank. You think I'm gonna go to some expensive-ass school and not take advantage of every single opportunity that comes my way? I work at my school's summer camp, I help coach the middle-school wrestling team, and I tutor on the side."

I don't care if he sees me raise my eyebrows and look at him differently now. Sure, I was sold on the whole private-school thing, but now that I know that he works hard for his money, I don't mind this cab ride at all. "I'm not trying to get into your pockets, though," I say, just so we're on the same page.

"I know. Like I said, you're not just some girl from around the way. Trust me, I can spot a gold digger from afar. But once they find out that I get my money from wrestling and tutoring, they usually kick me to the curb." He eases his hand toward my thigh and rubs his knuckles against my jeans.

I laugh and slap his hand away. "No they don't. Girls from around here . . . as long as you look good and can take them to Red Lobster . . ."

"I hope you're not expecting Red Lobster from me."

"I wouldn't mind . . . a MetroCard for the subway, a good movie, some cheddar biscuits, and I'm good."

"Oh, is that all it will take?"

"What do you mean 'Is that all it will take'? I know what you're thinking, so no! I might just want Red Lobster, and that's it. Ain't no tit for tat in that!"

He side-eyes me again, as if to ask me if I'm sure. At that same moment, something settles in my belly and I need to remind him that this is not a date. "We're just chillin', right? I mean, you're cool and all, so I wouldn't mind getting to know you." So we have small talk on the whole ride to downtown. Well, he has small talk. In half an hour, I know all about what it's like to be the best-looking black guy at the Easton School. When he says this, I immediately think of Darius. I don't want to, but he pops into my mind, and I start comparing the two of them.

As for looks, Darius wins for being almost perfect, like a model, as if he's been Photoshopped with that smooth brown complexion and a symmetrically angled jawline. But he's almost too pretty and stuck-up for my taste. So Warren takes the prize for overall swag—handsome with a little edge, some rhythm to his walk, bass in his voice, and he laughs at his own jokes.

I pretend to laugh too, but the passing buildings and streets out my side of the window are competing for my attention. I want to ask him about the set of new condos going up on

Fulton Street. I want to search the newly rounded street corners for the old Rasta man with the white beard who used to sell colorful rugs, old wooden furniture, and even used pots and pans in an empty lot. I want to know what happened to the row of wood-framed buildings that were sandwiched between a day-care center and a grocer. We're driving through Bed-Stuy and Clinton Hill, and these neighborhoods are like my face and body when I was in middle school—familiar but changing right before my eyes.

"Personally, I don't know why they moved to Bushwick in the first place," Warren continues.

I'm pulled back into his small talk, didn't realize that it had turned to Darius. "Why does he say he moved to Bushwick, anyway?"

"I don't know. We don't chill like that." He shrugs.

"You're cool with Ainsley, though, right?"

"He's cool. They're both cool. It's just that there's not really much we can talk about. We don't have anything in common. There's some other brothers in the school that I roll with. But not Darius."

"I feel you. Trust me."

"I see Janae's all up on Ainsley."

"No. It's the other way around. My sister doesn't get down like that."

"You're different from Janae, right?"

"Yeah. Wait. What do you mean by different?"

"You wouldn't go for some dude like Ainsley. Those bougie dudes who think they're better than everybody. Especially *Darius*," he says, smirking. "I can tell you like guys you can relate to. A little hard and with a little edge."

"You can say that again." I laugh.

He laughs too, at some inside joke we haven't even shared. I side-eye him because clearly, he's got game.

We get to our destination, and I assume we're going to the movies because it's just a couple of blocks away, but we're headed down Montague Street, a part of downtown Brooklyn I've never really been to. Brooklyn is segregated like that. There are definitely parts that are not hood, like Montague Street in Brooklyn Heights, but all kinds of people walk through here for whatever reason. I never have. The stores are too expensive, there are no basketball courts or handball courts, no bodegas or front stoops to roll out a barrel grill for jerk chicken, no pastelitos in deep fryers in small, smoky kitchens, and no crowded apartments filled with aunties, uncles, or cousins from Haiti or the Dominican Republic.

"You've been to the Promenade before?" Warren asks, taking my hand.

I gently pull away and pretend he didn't do that in the first place.

I have to decide in a split second whether or not to let

Warren know how sheltered I am. There aren't many places in Brooklyn my family and I have ventured into. A big shopping trip is taking the B26 bus down Halsey Street to the Fulton Mall. And when we do take a cab, it's to the Brownsville BJs in Gateway Mall or to Costco in Sunset Park. Going to Manhattan is a treat. I can count on one hand how many times we've been to Times Square.

Mama and Papi are either always working or always tired— Papi with his two jobs and Mama with us and the housework. So we mostly stay in the hood, where we can just walk around on our own and everybody knows us.

"Yeah, I've been to the Prome-whatever," I say.

"Well, that's where we're going. It's my favorite spot in Brooklyn."

"Oh, really?" is all I say.

"You know, that's kinda what I wanna do with the kids in our neighborhood," he says, almost reading my mind. "Take 'em on field trips. I bet you a lot of them ain't never been to the Empire State Building or even Harlem. That was the case for me."

"That'll be really cool. Make it big and give back to the community," I say really calm, but my heart is doing backflips. I never had a checklist of what I would want in a boyfriend. That was more Janae's thing. But as Warren talks, I'm making a mental list and checking it off at the same time. One: fine as hell. Check. Two: smart as hell. Check. Three: dreams, goals, and aspirations. Check, check, check.

Though I should take off points for how he keeps glancing down at my butt.

I wonder if this Promenade is expensive or if we'd both be out of place, but Warren seems like he can handle being anywhere, even with his diamond studs and sneakers. "Next time I'll take you to my favorite spot, other than the corner of Jefferson and Bushwick," I say.

"Where's that?" he asks, walking a little too close to me.

"The corner of Fulton and Hoyt. Downtown. It's where I buy my books," I say. "My father takes me there every once in a while."

"A bookstore is your favorite place?" He turns his whole body to me now.

"It's not a bookstore. It's a book . . . spot. This guy sells books on the corner."

"Why don't you go to a bookstore?"

"Well, it is like a bookstore. Come on, Warren. You know this already. You're smart, and if you didn't go to that fancy school, you'd be getting your books from the brother on the corner too."

"You like to read?"

"You're assuming that I don't?"

"I never said that. I just didn't think your favorite spot in all of Brooklyn would be a corner where some guy sells books. Why not . . . the library?"

"I like owning my books."

He pauses for a second. "I like you," he says.

I only half smile, hoping that he knows that I'm not falling for his game. But still, I kind of don't mind it. "You a'ight."

"Oh, I'm *a'ight*? I hear you, ZZ."

As he says this, the block we're walking on comes to an end, or rather, it opens up into a park, and in the short distance is New York City's skyline against a dim blue sky and faded yellow sun. We walk through the park, and I quickly realize why this is his favorite spot in Brooklyn. This park, or promenade, is right along the river separating Brooklyn from Manhattan.

Benches are lined against a metal fence, and the gray-blue water immediately draws me in. A warm summer breeze blows, and tiny bumps form on my arms. This is what Madrina calls grains of sugar adding sweetness to my soul; the first sparks of love and attraction, of something so new and tender that if I'm too firm with it, it will burst. I tighten my jaw and cross my arms to harden my stance and make everything about me firm and closed off.

This is not a date. This is not a spark of anything sweet, or tender, or shimmery. This is just me getting to know a boy named Warren from Bushwick. And that breeze is just giving me goose bumps. That's all.

"Want some ice cream?" he asks.

"Yes," I respond, without even thinking twice, and he places his hand in the small of my back and pulls me toward an old-fashioned ice-cream cart with a white man wearing a white apron and a chef's hat. I ask for chocolate. He asks for butter pecan.

We eat our ice-cream cones and walk and have more small talk about the program he went to, how he learned to skim through boring books and still ace the tests, the rich white kids he knows, wrestling scholarships, and the connections he's already made at Easton. I don't talk. I listen.

And this thing we're doing, in this place at the edge of a river with buildings and row houses on one side, and the city-scape on the other, is just chillin'. It's that warm spot on the couch when my favorite show is on TV. It's a plate of Mama's food left out for me on the table and covered with a paper towel for when I get home from school. It's our front stoop on a Saturday afternoon.

With this boy named Warren, home has extended out to this part of Brooklyn too—no matter how many fancy build-ings with doormen, expensive slices of gourmet pizza, and older white people looking at us with puppy-dog eyes there are. Still, we're just two homies from the hood getting to know each other.

"The Benitez sisters have a reputation, but not that kinda reputation," Warren says, bringing me back to the moment as we head back home. We walk up Jefferson Avenue from the L train. "Word on the streets is that Papi Benitez carries around a machete just to keep guys away from his daughters."

"My father does not carry around a machete." I laugh. "He doesn't have to. Me and my sisters don't get down like that." I accidentally bump into him. I remember that this is what Janae and Ainsley were doing at the park—purposely bumping arms.

We reach the corner of my block, and I have to decide if he crosses that line between my block and my front door. My block is my block and any- and everybody can come chill on our stoop. But bringing a boy to my door is a whole other level. I remember how Darius brought my laptop over, and I didn't think twice about it then because he was nothing and it was nothing.

But this is something. Warren is something.

We're already on our stoop, and I take the first step. I don't look up to see if any of my sisters are looking out the window, or if Madrina is at her window, but I somehow know that she sees me, even if she's deep in her basement with a client or going over her songs and prayers.

I stop on the second step and I turn to him, a few inches taller. "Well, thank you for walking me to my door."

He laughs. "You need to raise the bar, Zuri. Of course I'll walk you to your door. And I suggest you don't trust any guy who doesn't."

"Oh, you're schooling me on other guys now?"

"I'm just sayin'. But I plan to be around for a while, so get used to this."

I don't say anything to that. I don't protest. I'm soft now, like Mama's sweet, warm pound cake. And he's close enough to kiss me, so my heart starts to beat faster like conga drums, and I hope that no one is looking out the window; I hope that I'll know exactly what to do when his lips touch mine; I hope he steals a kiss quickly, while I'm standing here, waiting, breathing, with my heart pounding.

"So I'll text you tomorrow, a'ight?" He steps back with his hands in his pockets.

I frown, confused.

He keeps stepping back until he's completely out of our front gate. "Later, ZZ."

He holds two fingers up, then puts his hand back into his pocket and turns around. Just like that, he walks away, and I feel like the biggest idiot in all of Bushwick. I want to drag him back to this stoop and have a complete do-over. *I'm* supposed to be the one to turn away while *he's* waiting for a kiss. Not him!

"Bye, Warren!" someone calls out above me. I know it's Layla without even looking up.

From the corner, Warren turns around and waves to my sister.

"Come back soon, okay?" Layla calls out again.

Clearly, he's used to getting unwanted attention from girls too young for him, and maybe even girls too old for him. Or from girls, period. So he knows exactly what he's doing by just walking away like that. And it works.

I just stand there with my arms crossed, not ready to go back upstairs and face my sisters. That's when I see Darius walking up to his door while looking back at our building and rubbing his chin. He must've seen me. He must've seen Warren.

I smile to myself, watching Darius fumble for his keys. I'll be seeing Warren again, for sure. And that's when I'll steal the ball and take it to my court. This game is still mine. And Darius will be watching from the sidelines.

TEN

IT'S ALMOST A hundred degrees outside, and Charlise is dressed in a white button-down shirt and black pants as if she's coming home from a job on Wall Street. But she works a few blocks away at a new restaurant.

"You look like a butler," I say as she sits on the stoop next to me.

It's too hot to do anything else. Back in the day, we used to turn on the fire hydrant and run through that cool water as it flew up into the air and flooded our whole street. But Robert and Kyle threatened to call the fire department because it was a waste of water and taxpayer money, they said. Those two white boys who moved in down the block a few years ago have always had a way of making us feel bad for doing the things we love:

playing loud music, laughing from our bellies, yelling out our windows, and turning on fire hydrants when it's hot.

"I'm getting paid good butler money, though," Charlise says, as she unbuttons her shirt to reveal a black sports bra underneath. Something about the bra and the opened white shirt makes it look inappropriate, but Charlise is known for walking around the hood in just a sports bra, basketball shorts, and her Adidas sandals. She leans back on one of the steps and spreads her legs wide open, as if she's giving every part of herself some air.

At the same moment, Colin comes out the front door. We don't look back, but I know it's him, because I can smell the sweet cologne his aunt makes him wear. Madrina says it's to attract the right kind of girls—sweet ones who will be good to her beloved nephew.

"Whassup, ladies?" Colin sings.

I don't say anything to him while Charlise stands up from the stoop to let Colin pass. I want to tell her to button up her shirt because I'm sure Colin is staring a little too hard at her boobs right now.

"What's going on, Colin?" Charlise says.

"Chillin'. What's going on with you?" He steps closer to Charlise as if he's about to grab her hand, and this little exchange makes me raise my eyebrows, because Colin and Charlise used to hate each other when we were younger.

"I started working at this restaurant on Halsey. You should

come by sometime," Charlise says, and I raise my eyebrows even higher.

"Oh, a'ight. What are you, a chef or something?"

"I'm a hostess. And I hope you like asparagus."

"Yeah, whatever. Tell me when, and it's a date."

This time I look at them both with my mouth wide open. There goes that word again: *date*. "Colin, you're not gonna like any of that food," I say, but that's not really what I want to say. I want to tell him to stop flirting with my friend as if he forgot he used to chase her around with water balloons right after she'd gotten her hair done just so he could see her get mad.

"I'm open. I'll eat anything," Colin says, licking his lips and looking at Charlise up and down.

I roll my eyes hard as Charlise starts to laugh. "Colin, you're such a cornball!" I say.

"Not as corny as your boys across the street, though," he says, pointing his thumb back at the Darcy house.

"Word," I say.

"Word," Charlise repeats. Then she says, "Okay, then. I'll text you and let you know when you can stop by. I'll have a special meal waiting for you. Do you know what a prix fixe is?"

I turn and pop my eyes out at her, but Charlise just stares at Colin, smiling.

And when he leaves our front stoop and walks down the block with a little bop to his step while looking back at Charlise, I say, "I know you're not that thirsty."

"Actually, I am."

"Charlise. Are you serious?"

"No. Not really, but why can't I just mess around with him? He does it to a bunch of other girls."

"'Cause you're not a dude, Charlise. You'll get a bad reputation," I say.

"See? That's the problem. If we treat guys the way they treat us, then we'll get a bad reputation? That's messed up."

"Well, do you care about your reputation?"

She pauses, looks up at the bright blue afternoon sky, rubs her chin, and says, "My reputation for playing ball? Yep. My reputation for playing guys? Nope."

I want to say the same thing, that I don't care about my reputation. But I do, because I already have one. All my sisters do. We have to be careful about who we fall for, especially me and Janae. Just because guys from around the way like us—even if we don't give them no play, it's still easy for them to talk shit about us. Papi is watching us, but so is the rest of the neighborhood.

I glance at the house across the street and fold my arms across my chest, as if I just opened up my shirt to reveal my sports bra too.

"Yeah" is all I say, knowing that I would make myself into a soft cushion for my dear sister to fall onto if that boy Ainsley pushes her too hard. I will never let anyone break her heart. Then I wonder, who would be my cushion? Who would try to push me? And who would I fall for?

Pride Comes before the Fall
(Haikus)

If I fall in love
Will I sink to the bottom
And swallow water

Make my belly full
With hopes of tender kisses
Round like the moonlight

High over Bushwick
Playing Cupid with our hearts
I am the archer

Later in the afternoon, I have to pass some of Colin's boys when I go into Hernando's. They know not to holla at me the same way they do to the others girls around the way. But I know they look. I can feel their eyes on my butt when I pass. I usually stick my middle finger up behind my back, and they laugh and say, "Yeah, that's Beni's daughter, all right."

Without fail, every time I come into Hernando's, he sings my name at the top of his lungs. "Zuri-loooze! Qué pasa, muchacha?"

"Whassup, Hernando?" I say, rolling my eyes, because I

swear he owes me like a hundred dollars from years of not giving back the right change.

I'm only here for a bottle of ice-cold juice, something sweet and chewy, and something salty and crunchy. And five of each so I don't have to share with my sisters who have all gathered on the stoop with Charlise for a game of cards. As I put all the snacks onto the counter, my phone buzzes. It's a group text from my sisters:

He's coming into the store!

I immediately know who they're talking about. So I text back.

So?

Darius looks surprised to see me in there, and he quickly looks away. He's so obvious, it's not even funny. We haven't talked since the Bushwick Riot concert at the park.

"Hey," I say.

"Hey," he says, and stands in front of the counter next to me.

"Eyyy! Rich boy!" Hernando says.

Darius purses his lips and looks down.

Part of me wishes that Darius would speak up if he doesn't like something, or else the guys around here will tear him to pieces. He can't let it all show up on his face so that they don't misinterpret his expressions. Our neighborhood is loud, and the people are even louder with their thoughts and opinions.

A smooth, old-school R&B groove is playing in the

background, and it makes this whole situation weird, as if this is a music video and Darius is the star and I'm just an extra. He's that well put-together. Again, he's wearing a button-down shirt and too-tight khaki shorts. I can tell that they're not the ones from the day we went to the park. These are *cargo* khaki shorts, and I want to kick myself for noticing that detail. I mean, doesn't he have chillin' clothes?

"Would you like a picture?" he asks with a half smile.

And I jump on the inside, not realizing that I was staring that hard. "No," I quickly say, feeling stupid for letting him catch me like that.

"Do you have any pencils?" he asks Hernando.

"Pencils?" Hernando says. He grabs a pen tied to a string and hands it to Darius.

Darius sighs and shakes his head.

"You need, like, one pencil?" I ask.

"Do you sell a box or a pack of pencils?" Darius asks Hernando again, while ignoring me.

"Nah, you gotta go on Broadway for that. The ninety-nine-cent store," Hernando says, stroking Tomijeri as he strolls onto the counter with his fat, furry body.

Darius steps back as if Tomijeri is some sort of alien creature.

"What? You're afraid of bodega cats?" I ask, smirking.

"Maybe I'm allergic to cat dander and I'd like to buy a banana or something. Don't you think that's grounds for a lawsuit?"

Both Hernando and I laugh out loud, and Darius immediately drops his head and shoves his hands into his pockets. He stands there for a long minute until three of the corner dudes come in and my heart skips a beat. All their eyes are on Darius as they walk in and even as they pass him, and one purposely bumps into him.

"Sup, Z?" one of guys says. It's Jay, who I've known forever. He doesn't take his eyes off Darius.

"What up, Jay? What you been up to this summer?" I ask, just to ease the tension. His other boys are getting drinks out of the coolers in the back.

From the corner of my eye, I can tell that Darius doesn't know what to do. He's looking at the stuff on the wall behind the counter as if he can't decide on something. But there's nothing but batteries, lighters, cigarettes, condoms, and such. Hernando is on his phone now, with Tomijeri curled up under his hand. Jay and his boys are talking shit, and they're extra loud. I know exactly what they're doing. So I tap Darius's arm and motion for him to leave with me.

"Ay yo, Z?" Jay calls out again. "I heard you were chillin' with my boy Warren the other day."

"That's none of your business, Jay!" I grab the plastic bag of snacks and make my way out of the store, hoping that Darius is behind me.

"What you mean that's none of my business? That's my boy."

"Bye, Jay!" is all I say.

"Should I let Warren know that you chillin' with this dude right here?" Jay says. I can tell by how close his voice is that he's following us out of the store.

I turn to see Darius right behind me, so I ask, "Darius, don't you go to school with Warren?"

"Yeah," he says, and his voice is much deeper than usual.

Then I poke my head around Darius and say, "Mind your business, Jay."

The guys fall back, and I'm relieved. They know not to mess with me, but I'm worried that if Darius is ever by himself in that bodega, they will definitely start some shit with him.

We're at the corner waiting for the light to change, and Darius is standing beside me, thank goodness. I try to see his face from the corner of my eye. "Were you gonna let them mess with you?" I ask.

"*Mess* with me?"

"Yeah. They were gonna start shit and you were just gonna stand there, right?"

He doesn't say a word as we cross the street and walk back toward our homes.

"You can't walk around here thinking that you're better than everybody else. These guys will put you in your place."

"Is that a warning?" he asks.

"No. That's good advice." We reach the corner of his house, and I can tell that my sisters are pretending not to be watching us.

"Thanks, but no thanks. I can handle myself just fine."

I laugh. "From what I can tell, you don't know anything about street code."

Now he looks at me dead-on. He's not smiling. His jaw is not moving. So I stop laughing.

"Why? 'Cause of my clothes?"

"Come on, Darius. If a bunch of guys walk into the bodega, you gotta acknowledge them. A nod, a whassup, a dap. Something. Anything. You don't just stand there and pretend they're invisible. And if your boy's name comes out their mouth, you gotta defend him. That's street code."

Now his jaw moves at the mention of Warren; he shifts his weight from one foot to the other. He blinks and looks every which way.

He inhales deep and says, "Where can I get pencils around here?"

"You mean you don't have no pencils in that big ol' house? No office supplies? No things you *need*, like pencils?"

He inhales. "No."

"Ay yo, Kayla!" I yell out to my sister across the street. "You got any pencils?"

Kayla immediately runs inside the house.

"Thanks," Darius says.

"You draw or something?"

"Yeah. But I need a number-two pencil to take a practice test."

"You're in summer school?"

"No. SATs." He's not looking at me. He cocks his head back as if he's annoyed that I'm still here with him. "Warren is in summer school. But you know that already, right?"

I raise my eyebrows, because that's definitely shade thrown at Warren. "Yeah," I lie. "So you've known him since the seventh grade, huh?"

"Yeah" is all he says, then turns away as if he's done with this small talk.

I could walk away because he's clearly annoyed with me right now, but if he doesn't want me here asking him a bunch of questions, then that's exactly what I'll do. "SATs, huh? You're gonna be a senior?"

"Yeah."

"But isn't it a little late? I took mine in the spring."

"You had a perfect score? Or close to it?" he asks, looking toward Kayla as she crosses the street.

"No. It was okay. Enough to get me into Howard."

"Well, I'm trying to get my best score," he says.

"'Cause you're trying to get into *Harvard*, not Howard, right?"

He starts to say something, but Kayla reaches us and hands Darius a few pencils with a big smile on her face. In no time, Layla is crossing the street behind her, just to be nosy.

"Harvard? No," he says. "Thanks for the pencils."

He starts to walk back into his house, but I can't think of

anything more to say. I'm not ready to let him leave yet. I'm still talking. I want to be the one to end this conversation. I want to ask him what schools he's applying to, but I don't want to look thirsty, especially with Kayla and Layla standing there looking at me as if I'm about to make some moves on this boy, when it's the furthest thing from my mind. But he suddenly turns around and walks closer to us.

"Kayla?" he asks while pointing to Layla.

"Guess again," Layla sings.

Then he points to Kayla. "Okay, Kayla?"

She nods.

"Kayla and Layla," he says, pointing to the right ones. "Sorry about the other day. It's just . . . I didn't feel like dancing."

The twins are beside themselves. They trip over each other trying to reel Darius into a conversation.

"That's okay! I mean, you don't know us like that."

"But can you dance, though? If not, we're gonna have to show you."

"Don't worry, there'll be another block party."

"You can dance with Zuri next time."

I give Layla a death stare, and I roll my eyes at Darius, just to make it clear that I still can't stand him.

Darius puts his hand up as if to say he's had enough. He smiles and nods his head to excuse himself. In no time, he's at his front door, and he walks into his house without looking back.

And my sisters and I are still standing there like three thirst buckets. I shove the plastic bag of snacks into Layla's hand and grab both their arms to cross the street. They can't wait to give Marisol and Charlise the lowdown on how Darius apologized to them, but I head straight into my bedroom. I glance out my window at the mini-mansion across the street, and I spot Darius stepping closer to the wide window on the second floor of his house. I step back away from view so he doesn't see me too. He's staring down, moving his head about as if looking for someone.

I smile—I can't help it.

ELEVEN

IT'S SUMMER VACATION, and Mama never gets up before we do when there's no school. I'm usually the first one to wake up. Well, the first one after Papi, if he has to go in for an early shift at the hospital. But this morning, Mama barges into our bedroom and turns on the lights.

"Y'all are not gonna believe this!" she sings as she shuffles in, holding a white envelope.

I prop myself up on my elbow. I'm on the bottom bunk, so there's no sitting for me. Janae just rolls over, Kayla opens one eye, Marisol is fully awake, and Layla doesn't move one inch.

Mama sits her big bottom on Janae's bed and fidgets with

the envelope in her hand. I look at her face to see if whatever is in that envelope is good news or bad news. She's grinning from ear to ear, and her eyes are wide and bright.

Mama gives Janae a kiss. "This is all 'cause of you, sweetheart!"

I roll out of the bed and sit next to Mama. I spot gold fancy lettering on the envelope, but Mama is moving around too much for me to see the full words.

Janae is sitting up now, and Mama hands her the envelope first. All my sisters have gathered around on the floor, because Mama is cheesin' hard and is clasping her hands as if this envelope is about to change our lives.

But Janae's face tells a different story. She doesn't jump out of bed and squeal. She doesn't clap and run out of the bedroom to tell Papi, like she did when she got her acceptance and scholarship letter to Syracuse. She just smiles and clutches the envelope to her chest.

"What is it?" I finally ask.

Layla tries to take the envelope from her, but Janae holds it tight.

"Is it money?" Marisol asks.

"Is is it a scholarship?" I clarify. "Or a study abroad thing?"

"Is it a love letter?" Layla asks.

Mama takes the envelope from Janae, pulls out the letter, steps into the middle of the room, clears her throat, and begins, "We, the Benitez family, have been invited . . ." She turns up her nose and pokes out her lips as if pretending to be fancy. "To a cocktail party." She says this in a fake British accent.

All my sisters laugh.

"A cocktail party?" I ask.

"A *cocktail* party," Mama repeats with an even worse British accent.

The twins laugh even harder. "Cock! Tail!" Layla shouts, holding her belly and slapping her thigh.

"Wait a minute. Who invited us to a cocktail party?" I ask, because we've been invited to parties before—birthdays, weddings, funerals, graduations. But none of them have ever been called a *cocktail* party.

"You need a cocktail dress for a cocktail party," Janae says, ignoring my question. She goes over to our shared tiny closet and pulls out dress after dress.

"Do you need a cock and a tail too?" Kayla laughs. She and Layla give each other a high five and I want to throw a shoe at them to make them shut up.

I finally grab the envelope from Marisol and read the whole thing out loud. "Dear Benitez family. You've been cordially invited to the new Darcy residence for cocktails, dinner, and lively conversation."

"I knew they were gonna have a party in that house!" Layla squeals. "Now we get to see it too!"

"Should I bring the chicken or the pork?" Mama says. "Or maybe they like finger foods. How 'bout some tiny pastelitos?

Or some fried plantains? I knew those rich folks were gonna come here and bring some good luck with them!"

The next Saturday we arrive at the front door of the Darcy house. Janae is the one to ring the bell, because according to Madrina, she's the one who has led us all to this door in the first place.

I'm dressed in a plain denim skirt, flowery top, and a pair of Janae's sandals. I look like I've made the least effort for this party compared to my sisters, who are dressed like they're heading to prom.

"I'm gonna need some company in case Ainsley's busy with guests or something," Janae had said. "Please, Zuri!" By coming here, I took one for the team, for the fam, for my dear sister.

I don't smile when Mrs. Darcy greets us. Her eyes immediately drop down to our shoes. So I look down too, to see Mama wearing her leopard print platform stilettos that she bought for her fortieth birthday party at a small club in Bed-Stuy. My face gets hot with embarrassment because I knew that this wasn't the kind of party for those kinds of heels.

Mr. Darcy shows up behind her, and it's only then that she opens the door wider.

"Welcome, Benitez family!" Mrs. Darcy sings in her strange accent. It's British, but not quite white people British. It's kind of bootleg fancy, like a knockoff Louis Vuitton bag. This is the closest I've seen her, and she looks more like a big sister to Ainsley and Darius than their mother.

Mrs. Darcy's face drops when Mama hands her the aluminum pans. Mama clears her throat. "A preview of my catering business!" she says too loudly. "The top one is pastelitos. I learned how to make them from my husband, Beni. Since I ain't Dominican and all, I had to learn how to cook that food to keep my man!" She laughs, and her voice echoes throughout the room full of people.

"And the bottom pan has griot—Haitian fried pork. I'm Brooklyn-born and raised, but Haitian all the way. You see my daughters? Look at their figures! That comes from the good cultural foods we feed them. No skinny minnies in my house! You should have some griot," my mother says, looking down at Mrs. Darcy's fitted sundress. "Where your people from?" Mama talks a mile minute without even giving Mrs. Darcy a chance to say a word before she strolls into the living room with her heels click-clacking on the hardwood floors. Marisol and the twins follow right behind her.

"London. My people are from London. A neighborhood called Croydon," Mrs. Darcy says to us, because Papi, Janae, and I are still standing there waiting to be invited in.

We just nod before Mr. Darcy shakes Papi's hand and gently pulls him inside. In a second, both Janae and I are back in the Darcy house, and we can't believe how different it looks and feels with soft music playing in the background, the hum of voices, and people. Different kinds of people. There's a mix of black and not-black, white and not-white, and everything in between. Everyone looks really neat and polished. I look down at my own clothes. My skirt looks old, like it's from a whole other decade. Then I remember that it's actually Mama's from when *she* was in high school. The stitching from my sandals is coming loose, my toes are crusty, and my knees are ashy. I want to run back home and change. Actually, I want to run back home and stay there.

But Janae and I both spot *them* at the same time, and my sister grabs my hand and squeezes it. Ainsley and Darius. Darius and Ainsley. Their faces. Their shoes. Their clothes.

No guy in the hood wears bow ties. And suspenders. And dress pants so skinny and fitted, we can actually tell *how* their legs are bowed: slightly curved around the knees, as if they're Olympic runners. And they work out. It's easy to tell that they work out.

Janae leaves me behind as Ainsley takes her hand and walks her to a far corner of the room to introduce her to an older, good-looking black couple.

Now I really don't want to stay. I turn around to see that the front door is way too far, and I'd have to walk through the Darcy parents, as well as Mama and Papi, to get to it.

"Club soda or cranberry juice?" a person in all black asks.

I shake my head no.

But someone takes one of the clear, bubbly glasses and hands it to me. It's Darius. We're both silent as I grab the glass from him, our hands brushing. For a moment, I think he purposely touches my hand, because he smiles a little. I glance away, but when I look back our eyes meet. So I take a sip of the drink, then gulp down the whole thing out of pure nervousness.

"Slow down," he says. "I know it's not wine, but you can pretend." He gives me a smirk as the twins come to stand next to us. Layla is holding a glass of deep red liquid.

"Z, why you so corny? You should have *this* instead of that," Layla says, swirling the glass around while holding up her pinky. She takes a long sip and coughs. Kayla pats her back, giggling.

Out of the corner of my eye, I see Darius step aside to talk to someone else, and I'm both relieved and embarrassed.

"I thought y'all don't like cranberry juice," I say to the twins.

"It's not cranberry juice," Layla sings with a wide smile. "We're bad and bougie up in this bitch!"

"Layla!" I whisper-yell through clenched teeth, and try to grab the glass from her.

But she snags it back, and some of it spills onto her dress. I turn slightly sideways to see that Darius has his eyes on us. I grab Layla's arm to pull her away, but she keeps talking.

"I'm so glad Janae finally learned how to get a rich boyfriend. She better stay in his pockets so we can keep living this good life!" Layla says this loud enough for the people around to hear, possibly including Darius.

I pinch her arm so hard that she can't even scream. She knows that I mean business. "If you don't get your act together, I'm gonna tell Mama and Papi about all the times you cut school last year," I whisper in her ear.

Even Kayla's mouth drops open when I say this.

Another lady in black comes over and holds an empty tray out in front of me, and I grab Layla's glass and place it on the tray.

"What was that?" I ask her.

"Red wine," she says, and walks away.

Layla is holding her arm and covering the spot where I pinched her. Tears are welling up in her eyes while I give her the death stare. Well, it's more than a death stare—it's an I'm-about-to-hit-you-so-hard-you're-gonna-end-up-six-feet-under stare.

"And these are my twins!" Mama's voice sings from behind me, and Layla quickly fixes her face. "They're headed to the ninth grade. They're my pride and joy, and they're also giving me my premature gray hairs."

The twins quickly change their tune, because while I'll only pinch and stare at them, Mama will straight up call them out and embarrass them in front of all these people. Like how they just embarrassed me.

I look around the room for Darius, to see if there's any hint that he might've heard what Layla just said about Janae being a gold digger. I know that it's not true, but Darius is dumb enough to believe what comes out of my sister's big mouth. I spot him standing next to Ainsley, and they're both looking in our direction while Janae talks to Carrie. I quickly turn away, but I can still see them out of the corner of my eye. Ainsley's eyes are glued to us. Darius is whispering something into his ear, and Ainsley's face changes.

I recognize that look. It's that same look people used to give us when Mama would get on a crowded train with a double stroller holding the twins, me, Marisol, and Janae with our messy hair, runny noses, and each with a bag of chips to keep us occupied while Mama quieted down the babies. It's the look that assumes that Mama is a single mother, that she's on government assistance, that she beats us when she's tired, that we all have different fathers, that we live in the projects, and that we're ghetto. Everybody used to look at us like that—white, black, other mothers with kids who thought they were being responsible by only having two or three. I'd look back at them with defiance and a little pride; a look that says that I love my family and we may be messy and loud, but we're all together and we love each other. That's when I perfected my Bushwick mean mug.

Janae eases toward Ainsley. But his whole vibe has changed. I can tell that Janae is waiting for Ainsley to respond to something she just said. But he looks around as if this conversation is the last place he wants to be right now. So I walk over to my sister, worried that something is about to go down. And at the same moment, Ainsley says, "Please excuse me, Janae." He walks away, heading toward the kitchen, escaping.

"Ainsley? Where you going?" Janae asks.

"Hey, Nae-Nae, wait," I start to say, but I'm ignored as my sister brushes past me and goes running after him.

"Darius, what did you just say to your brother?" I say.

Darius just shrugs and says, "Clearly something that needed to be said."

"What—"

"You're a smart girl, Zuri. You'll figure it out." And with that, Darius walks away.

My stomach drops as I watch Janae say something to Ainsley with a confused smile. He says something without a smile. Her smile diminishes, but there's still hope in her eyes as she speaks. Ainsley shakes his head, shrugs, and places his hands on Janae's shoulders. He looks like he's both comforting her and holding her away from him at the same time. Janae's smile completely disappears. Ainsley mouths, "I'm sorry," before he slips into the crowd. And that's my cue to go over to her.

"Janae," I whisper while gently taking my sister's arm. Her eyes are welling up with tears. "What just happened? What did he say?"

"Zuri, let go. Please." Her voice is rough. She pulls away from me and pushes through the fancy people.

I swear on Madrina's orishas, if Ainsley has hurt her in any way . . . I turn to the Darcy boys and part of me wants to go over there and tell them off to their faces. But that's exactly what they would expect. I curse under my breath and follow my sister, my heart pounding in my ears.

Pretty Rich Boy

Hey rich boy, how much for that dollar?
    I need to buy a dream
I've gathered the clouds and stars
    to form a cheerleading team

Shouting "Shoot your shot!" from the sidelines
    thinking that if I win
They all have a turn at this wheel
    to take it for a spin

My mama wants to play too,
    but she's late to this game
A dollar is a dollar, she says,
    things are still the same

But if you sell me this dollar,
    I'll owe you three
Work myself to the bone,
    none left for family and me

Now, you got my three dollars
  with your dreams already paid for
Walking into fancy rooms,
  never kicking down a door

But you own that door, that room,
  that house, and its land
So I'd have to give you four more dollars
  just to pay for where I stand

If you could, you'd charge me for the air I breathe,
  the dreams I dream
Even the love I love, make my own beating heart
  turn on me like some scheme

TWELVE

I BRING SOME of the fancy food from that cocktail party up to the roof in a small container. Janae is already sitting cross-legged on the blue tarp, but she's facing the other direction, as if trying to avoid the house across the street. I don't blame her. So we face Hernando's bodega instead, where we can see some of the guys on the corner doing what they usually do.

It feels good to see them there. I've never known Hernando's to not have men sitting outside, young or old. Some people think they're up to no good, that they're wasting their time. But I think they're really there to look out for the block, for the whole hood, like gatekeepers. They know who's coming in and out; they know the faces of all the people who pass them.

Even with their big, fancy house on the corner, those Darcy

boys couldn't care less about what's happening on this block, much less this neighborhood. They bring outsiders to show off their house and talk about how much better they are than the people who are already here.

"I can't stand them," I say out loud.

Janae sighs long and deep. "You were right," she says.

"I'm sorry," I say.

"Me too," she says.

A long thread of silence keeps us connected. I know what she's thinking. She's replaying all the moments with Ainsley in her mind—what he said to her just now, but also the other times, how he made her feel, how he touched and kissed her. So I have to ask.

"Did you guys—"

"No." She cuts me off. "Z, he was a complete gentleman. I thought he was genuinely interested in me. We talked about everything. And we laughed a lot. He wasn't like any of the other guys out here."

"Huh. Clearly."

"He was really, really nice to me."

"Well, nice doesn't cut it, Nae. I'll take keepin' it real over nice any day."

"He was even nice when he broke it off."

"Broke it off? How exactly did he break it off?" I unwrap my napkin of tiny meatballs at the ends of toothpicks and hand one to Janae.

"He said, 'I'm just not ready for something serious right now,' and he didn't want to stop me from dating anyone else."

"He said that?" I ask.

"Yep. As if I'd even want to date anyone else."

I throw the tiny meatball stick back into the container and grab Janae's before she pops it into her mouth. I stand and walk close to the edge of the roof with the container in hand.

"Zuri, what are you doing?" Janae asks.

I ignore her and take one tiny meatball at a time and try to fling them across to the Darcys' roof. They don't quite land there, but I step back and try to throw the little things with all my might, one by one. "Take back your stupid, useless, tiny meatballs!" I yell.

When I turn to her, I catch Janae wiping her eyes. "Are you crying?"

"No," she says, and blinks back tears.

I sigh and go over to sit next to her and pull her in. I lay her head on my lap so I can braid the side of her hair. This always relaxes her. "You didn't know him that well, Nae."

"It's not that," she sobs. Now, she lets it all out as my hands rub her scalp. Janae has always been the sensitive one. If I start to tear up just because Papi's hard on me, Janae will straight up bawl at any hint of disappointing our father. "He was really different, Z. I mean, I met guys at school, and they were all right. But none of them were really interested. You know how many more girls there are than guys at my school? Lots. I didn't just wanna hook up with anybody. I wanted a real relationship. Nobody's trying to have a relationship their freshman year of college. And it felt like that was the direction we were going. And . . ." Her voice trails off.

"Janae, are you serious? Come on! What about your grades, focusing on getting a job right after you graduate? And us? Mama and Papi?" I ask, finishing a braid.

"Just because I like somebody doesn't mean I forget everything else in my life. People have relationships, Z."

"Yeah, but it's such a distraction. And if it doesn't work out, then it was a waste of time."

She gets up from my lap and looks at me. "So, you being with Warren is a waste of time?"

"No. We're just chillin' like I do with Charlise. Like we are now?"

"You know damn well that it's not the same."

"Lie down. I'm not done with your hair yet," I say, trying to change the subject.

"Zuri!"

"All right!" I sigh. "It's just that . . . I don't get you, Janae! Why do you have to fall so hard? And so fast? Ainsley was not right for you and I told you that. I knew this would happen."

We're quiet for a long moment before she asks, "How do you know? How do you know if the guy you meet won't be the one you spend the rest of your life with?"

I sigh again. "I don't think Mama knew that she'd still be

with Papi way after high school. Maybe they took it one day at a time. Like going up a flight of stairs or something. You take each step, and at some point, you land. You don't have to climb anymore. Or it stops getting so hard."

"We were still climbing, though."

"No, *you* were still climbing. He was on a nice tour of the neighborhood. You were all the way up those stairs, and he was still at the bottom snapping pictures and shit."

She shakes her head and sighs. "It didn't feel that way. I swear, even if it was just a couple of weeks, it felt as if we were both climbing while holding hands. He was so excited for me to meet his family, Z. He introduced me to his grandparents. He kissed me right in front of them. And then, out of nowhere, he did an about-face."

"I know exactly what happened. He met *your* family."

She purses her lips and furrows her brows, and I can tell that she's about to cry again. I let her. I don't look at her when she wipes her tears from her cheeks. I don't judge her. I know her too well for that.

But I'm judging Ainsley Darcy.

Janae cries herself to sleep that night, and I can't stand to hear it. Part of me hopes that she won't spend the rest of her life crying over boys, or men, who break her heart. One day, she'll have to toughen up. She'll have to be the hard candy shell to her own gooey sweetness.

I lie in my bed, wide awake, listening to the faint sound of drums coming from Madrina's basement. Tonight is one of her bembé ceremonies to celebrate some of her godchildren. An orisha will be called down tonight, and it will probably be Ochún. I slip out of my bed and tiptoe barefoot to the front door. I turn the lock open as silently as I can and make my way down to the basement.

Madrina grins at me as I walk down the crooked wooden stairs. It's cool and damp down here—the heat of summer held at bay. The room is crowded tonight with men and women from the neighborhood—some with their heads wrapped with white fabric like Madrina. They all smile when they see me. I recognize them from some of Madrina's consultations, and I know all their business. I find a spot in the corner to listen to the musicians build up the tempo so the spirits can get called down.

Bobbito is the master drummer for the ceremony. He sits on a folding chair with the huge bembé drum between his legs. He's bald, but he still wears a yellow bandanna on his head where sweat gathers along the edge. Next to him is the second drummer, Manny, a shorter man with a mustache so thick, his lips are invisible. Manny wears his yellow bandanna around his neck, and he's always in a white tank top, no matter how cold it is outside. And Wayne is Papi's good friend from way back in elementary school. These drummers have known me since I was a baby. And when I come down from upstairs, they always call me to dance to the drums. They call me the daughter of Ochún.

"Come sit near me. Don't hide," Madrina calls out to me.

She pulls a wooden stool close to her. She's pushed her consultation table into a corner, and on it are a half dozen yellow candles with their bright dancing flames. Her face glows a rich golden brown against her colorful beads and white head scarf.

Madrina can probably read it all over my face that I need to talk. "I'm worried about Janae, Madrina," I say as I sit down. "That boy broke her heart."

"Ah, sí. But what about your heart, Zuri Luz?" she says.

Madrina takes a cigar and lights it from one of the candles. She brings it to her red lips and pulls deep. When she lets out the smoke, it swirls and dances over all the candles as if performing for Ochún too.

"This isn't about me. Madrina, Janae was crying over some boy she just met."

"Who? The investor's son across the street? That's not just some boy, Zuri. He is a rich and charming boy. And very handsome, don't you think? All the fine things that are meant to seduce women." She inhales and exhales the sweet dancing smoke. "Do you think you are so different?"

I roll my eyes hard at that one. "Please, Madrina. Ain't nobody seducing me. And if someone is trying to get with me like that, then he can go 'head with his stank self." But my mind drifts to Warren and to Darius.

Madrina looks at me dead-on with a smirk. Bobbito is drumming a solo, and more people are trickling in. These things don't start until a little bit after midnight and some of these people work in the morning, including Madrina, who sometimes takes clients as soon as the bembé is over.

"Dance with us tonight, Zuri." Madrina squeezes my hand and I nod. Dancing in a bembé is something I've done since I was a little girl. The drumming sounds good, and so does Madrina's singing. I love feeling the beat of the drums in my body and letting go of everything as I dance.

I'm not dressed for this, but Madrina always has a wide, flowing white skirt for any newcomers to these ceremonies. So I pull one over my pajamas and it reaches my ankles. I dance barefoot so that I'm closer to the ground, closer to los antepasados, as Madrina says. There's also a pile of fabric for anyone to use to wrap their heads. Madrina says it's where the orishas enter. Tonight, it's Ochún who's supposed to fill our heads with thoughts and dreams of beautiful sparkling things, pretty faces, soft touches, warm hugs, tender kisses, and deep connections. So I wrap my head with plain white fabric because I want this Ochún out.

Bobbito, Manny, and Wayne find a groove; then in comes Madrina's bellowing song about Ochún, the Santería river goddess of love. And I begin to move like the water.

Dance of the River Goddess

if oceans are the wombs of the world
then I am the interconnecting
umbilical cord with deep love flowing
like the swirling hems of dresses
in dances for you goddess
and instead of sea salt I'm sprinkled
with golden dust to shimmer like the sun
because it loves me back even while beating
on my wrapped head like a tambora
and I am born hot and thirsty
panting at the edge of a river
wanting to submerge my head deep
within the bottom of the clear cool water

"Wépa!" Madrina sings.

I'm grinning from ear to ear now, because I didn't realize just how much I love dancing to drumbeat rhythms that pull at my core. I take the hem of my wide skirt with both hands and move it about like a wave. And with my swirling and flowing skirt and dancing body, I form a river. The drumming ebbs and flows, comes to a crescendo before stopping completely; then I am stagnant water again. Like all those tears I hold in and never let flow.

Everyone claps, and some even throw dollar bills at me. An offering.

"I hope this won't be your last dance, Zuri, daughter of Ochún," Madrina says, clasping her hands and smiling brightly at me.

Something brand-new stirs inside and all around me, as if I've been turned inside out. I immediately know that this was more than just a dance, and maybe Madrina was right all along. Maybe there is something real in these spirits.

There's a quiet humming of praise for Madrina. "Gracias, Madrina, gracias!"

I leave the basement. With my dollars bills in hand and Madrina's skirt still around my waist, I race up the stairs, past my apartment, and quietly slip up to the roof. My lungs are still reaching for the night air as the orishas embrace me.

THIRTEEN

WARREN BRINGS FLOWERS to my door. Papi isn't here to see him, and Mama and my sisters are visiting with neighbors down the block. Part of me wants to rush him away from here so I don't have to answer to my parents, but I know I need to introduce him to Mama and Papi at some point.

I take my favorite spot on the steps after he hands me the colorful bouquet I recognize from the Key Food on Broadway. So I side-eye him to let him know that game recognizes game. He can't play a playa.

"What? You don't like them?" he asks, trying to hold in a laugh.

"I just thought the flowers from the Key Food on Broadway were for the people on their way to Wyckoff Hospital," I say.

"Well, obviously I wasn't on my way to the hospital. Aren't you gonna smell them?" Warren asks. He's kind of dressed up with a button-down shirt, but not a Darius and Ainsley kind of dressed up. He looks smooth with a little bit of edge—crisp shirt, jeans, and almost-new sneakers. His fresh haircut makes the dimple on his cheek stand out.

I sniff the flowers and shake my head.

"You ever had a guy give you flowers before?" he asks. His phone keeps buzzing in his pocket, and he pulls it out to silence it. I see the name Alana before he shuts it off.

I give him a look. "Don't pat yourself on the back just yet, Warren. Flowers are cool, but we're still just chillin'."

He laughs. "A'ight, ZZ. Now, let's get off this block and *chill* somewhere else."

"How 'bout we stay right here," I say while looking up and down the block for any sign of Mama.

"Aren't you gonna get in trouble?" he asks.

"I'll get in trouble if we keep going out and you never meet my parents."

"Oh. So we're going out now?"

"I mean, literally going out. Like, leaving the neighborhood. My parents wanna know who I be rollin' with. And since you're from around here, maybe they already know your parents."

He laughs. "I doubt it. My mother and your mother were definitely not in the same circles."

"How about your father?" I ask.

"He's not from around here."

"Lemme guess. Locked up? Second family? Or maybe your mother was the side chick."

"Oh, I see you've already put me into a box and wrapped me in newspaper. And I'm the latest headline: 'Black Teen Boy from the Projects with Absentee Father Makes It into New York City's Top Private School,'" he says.

I nod. "Sounds about right."

We both laugh because we understand this secret language. We can swap stories of epic fights and neighborhood rivalries, the best ballers, and the longest-lasting couples. Last time we hung out, he showed me his EBT card and said that he's never done that before with any girl—shared that part of himself where people will make all kinds of assumptions about what life he had and what future is waiting for him.

"So," Warren says, pointing his chin across the street. "I heard your sister and Ainsley are getting serious."

I shake my head really hard. "Nope! Not anymore."

He laughs. "I knew it. *Them* dudes . . ."

"Them dudes, what? I hope you're not saying that he's too good for my sister."

"Too good for Janae Benitez? Hell, no! Quite the opposite."

I spot Mr. Darcy in the window, and then he quickly moves away.

"Let's walk and talk," I say, taking my flowers with me. I decide that Warren can meet my parents another time.

"After you," he says.

We get up from the stoop and head down Jefferson toward Broadway.

"Why didn't you say anything to me before about Ainsley?" I punch him lightly on the arm.

"Would you have believed me if I said, 'Yo, Z. He's gonna try to play your sister.' I saw her face that day. Her nose was wide open."

"You can say that again. And hell yeah I would've believed you. I already had my suspicions. Especially with Darius."

"Yo. Don't get me started on him."

"Please, start. 'Cause my fist got his name on it."

Warren stops walking and laughs really hard. "You're not getting ready to deck nobody. You're not a fighter, Z. You're a lover."

So I ball up my fist and punch him really hard on his muscular arm. "That's what you get for underestimating me."

But Warren doesn't even flinch. He keeps laughing. "The way you punch, I think I'ma have to fight your battles for you."

We continue to walk and I shove him again, but he doesn't even move. "Puh-lease! I don't need anybody fighting my battles! And you don't punch, you wrestle. Darius needs somebody to deck him in that tight jaw of his."

"Damn. What you got against Darius Darcy? I mean, did he break your heart too?"

"Hell, no! I am nothing like my sister in that department. I just don't like . . . his face."

"You're in the minority with that one. Trust me."

I shrug. "Whatever. It's one thing to look good, but it's another thing to walk around knowing it."

"Well, what's wrong with that? I walk around knowing I look good. Don't you?" He looks me up and down and licks his lips.

"Warren!" I shove him again and laugh. We reach Broadway, and a train is passing by on the overhead tracks. It's a cool, breezy summer day and everyone seems to be outside.

We head into Bed-Stuy along Jefferson. We're now in a part of Brooklyn where some of the brownstones are nicer. A few have For Sale signs in the front, while others are completely renovated. They look less like brownstones and more like museums.

"Real talk, though. Darius thinks everyone's beneath him. Especially me," Warren says, after being quiet for a while.

I stop and turn to him. "Spill the tea, Warren, 'cause if you tell me some shit about those boys that pisses me off . . ."

He laughs, then clears his throat. "I started Easton in the seventh grade. That's their upper school. And back then, there were only, like, seven of us. So me and Darius were cool from the jump, even though he was way too corny for me. In that school, the thing to do was playdates and sleepovers. So I'd go to his apartment in Manhattan a lot, and he practically begged his parents to come to my place, even though I told him about the shootings and drug dealers and shit. I even showed him how to walk down the block and keep his head up in case somebody rolled up on us. He thought it was all fun and games, like the stuff he sees in movies. But his parents were not trying to have their son spend the night with some financial-aid kid at his welfare-queen mother's roach-infested apartment."

"What? Did they say that?" I ask.

"They didn't have to say it. I knew that's what they were thinking. Me and D were cool for a while, but then I got into a fight outside school. And Mr. Darcy tried to get me kicked out. He thought I was a bad influence on his son. But the worst part of that was that Darius didn't even have my back. He was all about coming to my house and seeing how it is out here, but when he came face-to-face with that shit, he straight up violated. That's street code numero uno: Have your friend's back. Always. Ain't that some shit? He's black, but he ain't that black, feel me? The way we do it out here, if your boy gets into a fight, ain't you supposed to have his back? But instead, his pops tries to get me kicked out of Easton."

"Dang, Warren. That's messed up. I'm sorry you had to go through that. I didn't know the Darcys were that shady."

"The Darcys are bougie, but they don't like drama. They're real protective about their reputation. My mother had to come up to the school and practically beg for me to stay.

She threatened to sue for discrimination. After that, Darius wouldn't dare look me in the eye."

I shake my head as something inside me comes to a boil. I'm fuming. Those Darcys can have all the nice things money can buy, but they don't have decency or compassion. Now I'm especially glad it's over between Janae and Ainsley. Not only do I have my sister back for the summer, but I know the truth about that family across the street.

"I'm sorry, Warren. Really. What Darius did is not cool," I say.

In an instant, Warren's arm is around my shoulder, a little too quick. "I appreciate that, ZZ."

"Uh-huh, I'm sure you do," I say, but I don't move away.

We walk and talk some more, and by midafternoon, we make it back to Bushwick, where the sun is blazing hot and it's even louder than in Bed-Stuy. We run into a few people he knows and who also know me. We go into different bodegas for water, Icees, chips, sunflower seeds, and it's all as easy as the warm summer breeze. When we reach the corner of my building, Warren faces me.

Suddenly I can't look him in the face. Warren is smiling and trying to get me to make eye contact. But I keep turning away and laughing, and he keeps trying to get me to see him.

"I promise I won't hypnotize you, Z," he says while gently taking my wrists and pulling me in.

"Yes, you will!" I tease.

"My eyes won't hypnotize you, but my kiss will."

I stop fidgeting and finally look at him. He's grinning so hard that I can't help but laugh.

Finally I stop. But I don't let him make the first move. I keep avoiding him until I'm ready to kiss him. I move in when he's not looking, ready to plant a fat, wet one on his lips, but someone calls my name.

"Zuri!"

It's Marisol, coming down the block pushing a shopping cart with Layla and Kayla. I quickly pull away from Warren because I'm not gonna hear the end of this from now until eternity—me kissing a boy at the corner for the whole neighborhood to see.

Warren pulls on my shirt as a way of asking me to finish what I started. But I reluctantly step away from him to greet my sisters.

"I'll catch up with you later, Warren," I say with a half smile.

"Oh, it's like that?" he says.

"I said, I'll catch up with you later." I walk away and leave him standing there, waiting and wanting more of me.

FOURTEEN

"YOU THINK HOWARD will take a collection of poems in place of an essay?" I ask Janae as she's laid out on the bed as if someone has stolen all her joy, all her sweetness, and turned her into a stagnant pool of salty water. Even though Ainsley is out of the picture, he's still latched onto my sister's heart. Janae's not crying, but she's taking up a whole lot of space with her heavy sighs, and moping around as if she doesn't have her whole life ahead of her.

"No. You have to learn how to express your thoughts without any metaphors or flowery words," she mumbles. She's mindlessly scrolling through her phone. It's noon and she's still not dressed.

Mama's footsteps are headed toward our bedroom door.

"Zuri, I need you to go to the check-cashing place and get the money order for Madrina's rent," Mama says.

"Come with me, Janae," I say as Mama starts to walk away.

"Let her be, Zuri!" Mama calls out.

"Why, Mama? You want her to lie up in the bed all day? It's nice outside."

"She's recovering from heartbreak. Let her be."

"Are you kidding, Mama?"

"Don't worry. You'll catch it one day too, Zuri. Just leave your sister alone." Her voice trails off as she heads into the kitchen.

I exhale, shake my head, and stare at the lump that is my sister beneath the old Dora the Explorer sheets. "Oh, hell no, Janae! You're letting that stupid boy win. You gotta come out on top, big sis! Let him see that you don't care. Let's get outta here and make sure that you look extra cute. Come on, Naenae! Please!"

I shake her, but she doesn't move. I tickle her, and finally her salty self melts back into her gooey sweetness. She keeps laughing long after I stop tickling her. She laughs so hard, tears stream down her face while she sits up, bends over, and holds her belly.

I finally have my sister to myself. Our faces are fresh, our hair is done, her dress is flowing, my T-shirt is poppin', and we look cute as we walk through Fulton Mall in Downtown Brooklyn.

Guys were hollering at us ever since we stepped onto the B26 bus going down Halsey, then after we transferred to the B25 going down Fulton. Still, those guys are not flies and mosquitos. Most of them actually look really good. But Janae and I are focused.

We finished Mama's errands, and we have the whole afternoon to ourselves without our little sisters, even though they begged Mama to come with us. I had to tell Mama that I was taking Janae out to nurse her heartbreak.

We get a nice booth overlooking Flatbush Avenue at Junior's, and Janae insists that our meal is her treat.

"I saved up most of my money from working at the bookstore on campus," she says as she sips her milkshake.

"I can't wait to get a job," I say, stirring the ice cubes in my soda. "You know I put in my application to just about every store on the Fulton strip. I shoulda done what Charlise did, stay local and get those white people and their boutiques to hire me."

The waiter comes to serve our food. Part of me worries that we've ordered too much and that Janae may not be able to cover it all. And that worry shifts to other worries. Things I've held in the back of my mind. I wonder if Howard is the right decision, if they'll give me a full scholarship and financial-aid package like Syracuse did for Janae, if I should start dreaming about other schools too. Or what if I get to Howard and I don't like it? What if I want to come home?

"What's wrong, Z?"

I tell her. I let Janae know all my fears. I lay them out on the table one by one: change, quiet, money, college, job, space, family, home.

"Z," Janae starts. "Things are gonna have to change, and you just have to open up to it. My whole world opened up the day I took that Greyhound to Syracuse. It's like, I knew I wasn't going to be the same person after that. And all it took was a five-hour bus ride. I didn't realize how closed off from the world we were."

I sigh. "But what happens if I get into Howard and it's not for me?"

Janae cocks her head to the side and looks at me just like Mama does. "Then you should go visit."

"Visit where?"

"Zuri! Howard," she says.

My insides jump at the idea of going anywhere outside of New York by myself. By myself! But then reality sets in. "Even if Mama and Papi let me go, with what money?" I dip a Buffalo wing into a cup of blue cheese.

Janae pulls out her phone and spends a couple of minutes scrolling. I see her typing something.

She shows me her phone and I read the screen, confused. She's bought me a round-trip bus ticket to D.C. To Howard. For tomorrow!

I look up at my sister in shock.

"Just go, for a day. I'll deal with Mama and Papi."

"Really?" I can barely get the word out, I'm so excited. A whole day to myself, exploring Howard.

"Yes, really. What are big sisters for?"

Of course my whole family has to escort me to Times Square at the crack of dawn, where I'll be hopping on a six-o'clock bus to D.C. I am so hyped about this trip that I haven't slept. I keep this giant ball of joy inside me so no one takes it away.

I worry that Papi will change his mind any minute. He's concerned that I'll be traveling alone. "I wanna make sure they see my face. And I wanna look each one of those bus passengers in the eye," he says.

But Mama is excited. It's starting to sink in that she's about to have two "baby girls" in college.

Mama packs three Tupperware containers of food for me to eat on the bus, and foil-wrapped snacks to eat over the course of the trip. Marisol typed up a budget for me. I'm supposed to spread out the twenty bucks Papi gave me over the whole day.

And after waving to my family until the bus pulls off, I finally make it out of Manhattan.

I mostly stare out the window, watching this part of the country pass. New Jersey, Delaware, and Maryland.

I take selfies and pics of the fast-moving world to send to my sisters and Charlise. I text Warren, but he doesn't text back right away, like he normally does. The last text I got from him was from last night, telling me to have a safe trip. Him and our almost-kiss linger in my mind as the bus zooms toward D.C.

D.C. is almost like Brooklyn, but much cleaner with way fewer people crowded onto the streets. And less black and brown people too, though I wonder if they've been boxed in somewhere else, like in Brooklyn.

"D.C. used to be called Chocolate City," the woman sitting next to me says. She probably noticed how my face has been glued to the window for almost the whole ride.

"Well, I see a whole lotta vanilla," I say.

"Yep. I'm from Bed-Stuy. We're starting to see a whole lotta vanilla there too."

"Is that happening all over?"

"I don't know," the woman says. "I haven't been to all over. Have you?"

I don't answer her as the bus pulls into Union Station. From there, I take the Metro north, up to Howard University.

I walk toward the entrance, and it's exactly how I've seen it in videos and pictures. The brown brick buildings are regal. Giant green lawns spread across the campus. It kind of looks like Maria Hernandez Park, but without the playground, or the surrounding brownstones and buildings. Most important, without the new white people. There's just people like me, as far as my eyes can see. And it already feels like home.

* * *

All of Howard is clean and airy. No clutter. No sirens and loud music coming from outside. No bodega gates rolling up, and shopping-cart wheels on jagged sidewalks. Being here expands my whole world much farther than I could've ever imagined, and I text Janae one giant THANK-YOU in all caps followed by smiley faces, hearts, and balloons.

We have to meet our tour guides in the Administration Building. Inside, there's a long table with a sign hanging in the front that reads WELCOME TO HOWARD. Two girls are seated behind it, wearing big smiles and the cutest outfits I've ever seen. Their hair is done in long braids, and one of them has fancy designs on her nails. So I walk over to them.

"Hi, Zuri!" one of the girls sings after I introduce myself. "I'm Diane, and this is Sage. We're juniors here at Howard and we're student ambassadors."

Sage gets up to give me a hug over the table. "Okay, Zuri. About ten other prospective applicants will join us for a brief tour, and you can learn about Howard University," Sage says. While her hug felt real, that little spiel didn't. But I don't mind because this must be her job.

In just a few minutes, I'm surrounded by other kids who look about my age. Diane and Sage step away from the table and, with clipboards in hand, lead the group toward the other end of the yard.

"And here we have our Founders Library," Diane says as we approach a large redbrick building. "Built in 1939, it's open twenty-four hours a day, so there'll be no excuse to not get those papers in on time."

The library is majestic with its glowing white clock tower. I feel smarter just by standing in front of it. There's enough wide-open space for me to feel like I can actually chase my dreams here, and I'll be able to reach them too.

Diane and Sage then walk us over to the Tubman Quad. I think of Hope Gardens, back in Bushwick, with its quads too, but with less green grass and cleanliness, and less of just about everything. Thinking of the projects makes me think of Warren, so I snap a pic for him and text, *You might wanna rethink Morehouse and come to Howard.* I send a grinning face.

As we walk through the campus, I get to feel what it's like to be in college, to be in a place where new ideas and people will reveal themselves to me every single day. And not just any college—a historically black college, one of the first in this country. I wonder what the girls who've slept in my future dorm room over the years are doing with their lives right now. I wonder if they've gone back to their blocks or their towns and changed them in any way. I wonder if Howard changed them, and maybe they couldn't go back to their old hoods because they've grown too big, too tall. Not in size, but in . . . experience. In . . . *feeling.* I wonder how I'll change too.

After about a half hour of touring the lower and upper quads, some of the dorms, and the Cramton Auditorium, it's time to sit in on a lecture by one of Howard's professors.

As we finish our tour, some cute guys from across the yard call out, "H-U!"

Sage and Diane respond, "You know!"

Me and the other kids on the tour laugh and look around at each other.

"Y'all don't get to say that until you get accepted," Diane says.

But I whisper, "You know!" under my breath anyway as a sort of prayer.

We're back in the Administration Building, where Diane and Sage pull out another clipboard for us to sign up for a lecture. Fewer kids add their names for this one. Good. Less competition.

The lecture is on African American history, and the professor is someone I've read about online. Other high school students are here too. Not the ones who were on the tour. Suddenly my stomach is in knots. *This* is my competition. I look at my future classmates as we all walk through the campus yard toward Cramton Auditorium, where current Howard students will talk to us before Professor Kenyatta Bello starts her lecture. I wonder which of these kids I can rock with, and which ones I'll learn to stay away from.

We all spill into the giant auditorium, where there's a huge stage and screen in the front. Janae told me that some classes are held in auditoriums like this, and I'll have to always sit in the front to get the professors' attention. I do just that so I can be seen, noticed, and heard.

But other kids have the same bright idea, and the first few rows close to the stage are almost full. There's one last empty seat at the other end of the stage, and I head straight for it. This is musical chairs, and I'm trying to stay in the game.

But a girl places her hand on the seat's armrest, looks dead at me, and says, "Are you with Alpha Kappa Alpha?"

"Who?" I ask.

"The AKA scholarship group? These seats are reserved for them," she says with an even brighter smile.

"Oh" is all I say, even though I want to know what an AKA is and how I can get into their scholarship group. But I decide that girl doesn't need to know that—I can look it up online later.

A tall girl with flowing hair and a pink blazer walks over to the seat that should've been mine and sits down. I look around at the first few rows and notice that everyone's already teamed up. They're talking to each other and laughing, and I wish that I had brought one of my sisters with me. But still, I grab a seat near the back and stay focused. I didn't come here to make friends.

The first part of the session begins. I listen to every word those Howard students say about the different majors and clubs and activities the school has to offer. I hear about their newspaper, the *Hilltop*, and their literary journal, *Amistad*. I'm at the edge of my seat, and my heart feels like it's about to leap out of my chest from excitement. If only I could skip my senior year at Bushwick and move in, like, next week.

Sage joins the students on the stage to take questions from the audience. "Now keep your questions to just questions," she says into the mic. "No comments or reciting your application essay."

The audience laughs, but I don't. I'd be the one to recite my essay as a spoken-word piece if it would increase my chances of getting in.

I keep raising my hand, but Sage doesn't call on me. So I stand up and raise my hand high. I hear whispers around me, but I don't care.

"Yes," Sage says, finally noticing me. "With the afro."

A girl standing in the aisle with a mic passes it over to me. As soon as I take it, my stomach sinks, but I swallow back my fear. "Hi," I say, clearing my throat. "How can I get a scholarship to Howard?"

Everybody shifts in their seat, and some even giggle. My voice echoes, and my whole body goes warm. Still, I hold my head high and wait for an answer as the girl takes the mic away.

"Howard University reviews applications on a case-by-case basis. You can ask your guidance counselor for help. We look forward to hearing from you," one of the students on the stage responds.

It's an answer I already knew, but I sit back down and tell myself that I won't stop asking questions until I get in. I don't care how I look.

When Professor Bello begins her lecture, I take out my notebook to write down everything she says. Her words fill my ears, the students fill my eyes, and I have the overwhelming sense that I belong here. I imagine myself in this place, getting dressed for class, walking with my new friends to the dining hall, joining the poetry club. I sigh big and feel my body swell with hope about this new beginning. The professor keeps talking and I keep dreaming and I begin to write a letter to the founder.

Dear Mr. Oliver Otis Howard,

I wonder if when we name places
after important people, we've made them
immortal in some way. That their ghosts
can linger in corners and halls and dusty
dorm rooms to see me writing this letter
to some dead white man who probably could
never have imagined that I'd exist. Have you
heard of the Dominican Republic, Mr. Howard?
Or maybe you've heard about a slave revolt
that happened in a country called Haiti? These are the
places that made the people that made me. Those are
places that, in 1867, girls like me would not dream of being
in somewhere like your university. And this is why I want to

come to your school, Mr. Howard. There is more to learn
about my old, old self, and black and brown girls like me
from hoods all over this country want to
    take over the world,
but there's something missing
in our history books the public schools give us.
At least that's what my papi says,
so he makes me read a lot, and that's where I found out
about the Mecca in this book called

Between the World and Me

and I'm thinking that I need to come here so I can gather
these wisdoms found in old, dusty books written by
wrinkled brown hands and gather them within the folds
of my wide skirt, tuck them into the pockets of my jeans,
and take them with me back home to sprinkle all over
Bushwick like rain showers, Mr. Howard.

                        Sincerely,
                        ZZ

FIFTEEN

"HI, I'M SONIA," a girl says as she reaches for my hand to shake. We walk up the auditorium stairs and into the hallway. I see that she's about my height and my age. "Thank you for that question. Just about everybody up in here is trying to get a scholarship."

"Really? Oh," I say. "I'm Zuri, by the way."

We head out into the yard.

"Yes, really. You know how many people get in and can't pay? Some can't even finish," Sonia says.

"I hope that doesn't happen to me," I say. Fear settles in my belly like one of Mama's heavy meals.

"Well, you just gotta play your cards right. Get them grades up, and extracurricular activities are your ticket. Where you from, anyway?"

When she says this, I immediately think of my poems. I hope that's something that'll set me apart. I'm willing to use any skills I have to get into the school of my dreams. "Bushwick," I say. I rep hard for my hood wherever I go.

Sonia scrunches up her face.

"It's in Brooklyn," I add.

"Oh. Why didn't you just say Brooklyn?"

"'Cause Brooklyn is not Bushwick" is all I say.

"Oh, that's really cool. If you're from Brooklyn, then you probably liked Professor Bello's lecture."

"What's that supposed to mean?"

"I thought people from Brooklyn are extra woke or whatever. And besides, Professor Bello is from Brooklyn, or that's what I read in her bio. Bed-Stuy do or die, or something like that."

"Really?" I feel my whole soul light up when she says this.

"Yeah, really. You should really try to get to know her. She runs an open mic at Busboys and Poets."

We were walking toward the exit of the campus, but I stop dead in my tracks. "What did you just say?"

"An open mic at Busboys and Poets . . . it's a bookstore that's really close to here, if you want to check it out."

"How do you know all this?" I ask. The Brooklyn in me is not ready to trust this girl all the way.

"I'm from D.C., so I know all about Howard."

"Thanks, Sonia," I say with a genuine smile. If she's from around here, then she must be keeping it real with me.

"Nice meeting you, Zuri," she says. "Maybe I'll see you back here for freshman orientation."

I smile. "I hope so."

We wave goodbye to each other, and suddenly, a giant bubble of hope begins to well up inside me. I might just have a chance at this school.

"Busboys and Poets," I say out loud, and start to make my way off campus. I have just enough time to head over there before I need to catch my bus back to New York.

I walk out onto Georgia Avenue and take in the scenery: the shinier-than-usual cars, the well-dressed people, the wide, clean buildings. This part of D.C. is kind of like Brooklyn, but not Bushwick or Bed-Stuy, where everything looks old, used, and tired. Here, it looks as if people care—as if they're always expecting company, so everything has to look presentable for strangers.

I use my phone to find Busboys and Poets, and I step inside knowing that writers and poets come here to get their words right, to think big thoughts about the world, and to have deep talks like the ones Papi and his homies have on the stoop.

I'm drawn to the nonfiction shelf, where I try to find the thickest book of them all, no matter what it's about. It's a big book of art, so I hold it close to my chest, put my bag down, crouch down on a stepstool near the corner, and get lost in its pages. Mama texts me, and I send her a photo of the bookstore so she knows I'm safe and in a place I love. Layla sends me a silly meme, and I text her back a smiley face. I see that Warren has finally responded to my texts with a photo of him hanging out on my block, and I smile. Charlise sends me a pic of her and Colin, but I roll my eyes and I ignore it.

I pull out three more books; one of them is a poetry collection by Langston Hughes, and I read in his bio that this place is named for him because he was a busboy and a poet. I swim in his words until a voice talks over a microphone somewhere in another part of the restaurant. "Good afternoon, and welcome to Busboys and Poets!" he says. A few voices cheer.

My belly twists and my heart races, because time has slipped from me. I dig into my bag for my phone and see that it's five o'clock already. My bus leaves at seven. I'll need to get to the station in an hour, but I still have time to see what all this noise is about. I follow the voice that says he'll be inviting poets up to the stage in just a few minutes and advises anyone who wants to sign up to do so now, before they close the list.

My belly knots again, because his words are a command. There's no one here who knows me. There's no one from the hood who'll spread a rumor about me getting on the mic to spit some corny rhyme about love or the hood or my sisters. The last time I shared my poems in public was for the after-school performance in June, and even that was only for the kids who had taken that poetry class.

"Thank you all for coming out," the man continues. "We'll be featuring some local teen poets who were part of the Poetry Out Loud summer workshops. So give 'em a round of applause, y'all."

I walk to a separate part of the bookstore, where there's a restaurant, a small stage, and a black man wearing a bow tie. I only stand there and watch the people. It's mostly teens, all right. And I almost think of backing out. Strangers or not, and whether it's D.C. or Bushwick, I know kids my age can be brutal. Still, I'm drawn to the mic.

"But first let's get some of you young people to bless this mic," the man says.

There's a girl standing by the stage holding a clipboard. There's a short line, about five teenagers who walk up to her and sign up for the open mic. So I'm the sixth. Some people stare at me, I stare back. Others glance—I ignore them.

I write ZZ on a line, and I take a seat in a corner in the back of the room. A waitress comes to take my order. I have fourteen dollars left after I paid to get to the Howard campus, so I just ask for water.

Those few minutes before my name gets called go by like honey dripping from a spoon. And after each poet goes up, who are all just okay, the man finally calls my name. My heart doesn't race, my palms are not sweaty. I'm as cool as a snow cone.

The clapping is what gets me up from off my seat and adds

the rhythm to my slow walk toward the small stage, up the short flight of steps, behind the microphone, and into the lime-light. I begin to speak.

Girls in the Hood

Step onto my block
and walk these jagged
broken streets
and sidewalk cracks
like rickety bridges across our backs
to the ends of rainbows
reflecting off broken glass
where the pot of gold
is way on the other side
of this world.

So we hood girls
shout our pain
into the megaphone wind
hoping that it will carry
our dreams
to sky-scraping rooftops
with radio towers
broadcasting our tongue clicking,
smack talking, neck rolling

hip swaying, finger snapping
sass through telephone-wire
jump ropes while we skip to the beat
of our own songs and count out
the seconds, minutes, hours, days
until we break past these invisible walls
where glass ceilings are so high,
we only look up and never scratch the surface
with airbrushed and gel-tipped manicured nails
hoping that maybe
the stars will reach down
instead and want to touch us too.

My pulse races, and I can hear everyone start clapping. I can feel that my words have earned me respect. Just like when Papi sits with his homies on the stoop to predict a politician's next move, theorize some foreign country's strategy, or know who's about to have beef with who on the block weeks before something goes down. He drops knowledge just as he's slapping down a set of cards or a domino onto a table, and his homies can't do anything but bow down to his greatness and keep their mouths shut.

And I'm sure that's what everybody does as they applaud and cheer. That's when I know that this place can be an extension of my block too, like home.

I let myself get showered with applause and cheers before

I open my eyes again. And when I do, they land on a familiar face. That's when my stomach sinks. My breath quickens, and I'm frozen there on the stage even as the audience stops applauding and the man calls for the next poet to come up.

Darius Darcy is looking directly at me.

SIXTEEN

THE WORDS *WHAT the hell is* he *doing here?* play over and over in my mind. He's just standing there in the back of the room with his hands in his tight pants pockets. The late-afternoon sunlight shines on the side of his face, making him almost glow. We both have lights shining down on us as if we're the only ones in here.

Someone comes over to touch my arm, and I finally look away and step down from the stage. I almost don't know where to go, but then I remember I left my bag on the chair and I have to head over to where Darius is standing. I recognize one of the girls he's with. Carrie. This is not how I expected my afternoon to go. At all. And Darius just watched me perform? Oh, hell no.

"Small world, huh?" is the first thing Darius says.

"Too small," I say as I grab my bag without looking directly at him. "Way too small."

"So small, I'm starting to feel claustrophobic," Carrie says while shifting in her seat. There's an empty chair at their table that has Darius's bag hanging over the back, but I don't sit down.

"Wow, you all know each other?" the other girl asks. She looks familiar too, but I don't think I've ever seen her. Then I realize that she has the same square jawline as Darius. "Hi, I'm Georgia, and that poem was really good! Girls in the hood. I like that!"

"Zuri" is all I say, pretending to be uninterested because she really looks like Darius and I remember her name from when we were talking about that band at Maria Hernandez Park. She must be his little sister. The third Darcy kid.

Then Darius adds, "And guess what—Zuri lives across the street from us back in Bushwick."

Georgia gasps. "Oh my god! Wow! What a coincidence! What are you doing in D.C.? You go to Howard?" She sounds like her brothers—not her voice, but her words. No New York twang, no slang, nothing. She pronounces her words perfectly. She *enunciates*.

"No, I don't go to Howard. Yet. I'm a senior at Bushwick High. I'm just touring the campus for the day."

"Cool," she says.

Carrie doesn't say a word to me. She just smiles a fake smile and messes with her iced latte or whatever she's drinking. Another teen poet gets on the mic and yells so loud that I want to cover my ears.

"You're the last person I expected to run into here." Darius bends down a bit so that I can hear him. This is the first time I'm seeing him in jeans, I realize, but I don't stare too long. Our bodies are almost touching, boxed in by the chairs.

I nod, thinking about what Warren just told me about the Darcys. How Darius is shady, and I'm sure his sister is the same. But why does this D.C. Darius seem nicer than the one back in Bushwick? He's smiling more. His eyes are softer. His whole body language is more laid-back and chill.

"We've been wanting to get out of here to get some real food. Wanna come with?" he asks.

"Come with? No, thanks. I kinda wanna see the other poets," I say.

"No you don't. Trust me. You're ten times better than they are," he says, grinning.

"Totally. I can only take a little bit of that spoken-word stuff," Georgia says. "But you . . . *you* were amazing!"

I only smile because I see Carrie rolling her eyes. She catches me watching her, then flips her long straight hair over her shoulder.

"Thank you," I say to Georgia while keeping my eyes on Carrie.

"You still want those chili dogs, Darius?" Georgia asks.

"Heck yeah!" Darius says. He gently touches my arm. "I'm sure you didn't get a chance to go to Ben's Chili Bowl," he says. "You should really try it. It's good."

And I laugh. "Heck yeah?" I repeat, laughing. No one else is. Clearly they don't get how corny Darius sounds saying *Heck yeah*. "You eat chili dogs?"

"Let me guess," Darius says. "You thought those hors d'oeuvres at our party are what we eat for dinner every night?"

I shake my head and try very hard not to laugh again. "No, I didn't think that at all."

"Yes, you did, Zuri," he says. "And do you eat those fried pork chunks for dinner every night?"

"No, of course not," I say, and let out another laugh because he's right. And I was wrong. For the first time since meeting him, since hating him, I hear him laugh, too.

Georgia smiles while looking at her brother, then at me, then back at her brother. All the while, Carrie is dead serious.

We leave Busboys and Poets and walk around the corner to a place called Ben's Chili Bowl. It looks like it's been there since forever, but the surrounding buildings have been scrubbed clean and polished. It's a short red-and-white building that has giant yellow signs with red lettering and pictures of a hot dog and a hamburger. Inside feels like my Brooklyn—the familiar black women behind the counter wearing hairnets, plastic gloves, and warm smiles; the smell of food feels like a big hug from Madrina; and smooth R&B playing in the background makes everything seem as if it's swaying to the music. Whatever they serve here, both Papi and Mama would love this place. I imagine taking them here when they visit me on campus.

I stand back against the wall while Darius orders for his sister, then Carrie, and then he turns to me.

"No, thanks," I quickly say.

"You sure?" Georgia asks. "'Cause nobody from New York turns down anything from Ben's Chili Bowl."

I shake my head no even though I'm hungry as hell. I don't want to hang out with them longer than I have to. After a few minutes of waiting for the food, small talk, and watching Carrie try to shut me out by making sure she gets in between me and Darius every chance she gets, we end up sitting in a booth in the back. I sit next to Georgia while Carrie sits next to Darius, of course. I want to blurt out that I don't want her man, but it would be a waste of my breath at this point.

"My brothers told me that our new neighborhood is really loud. Good thing we have central air to keep out all that noise," Georgia says in between spoonfuls of her chili.

"It's not noisy," I say. "As a matter of fact, if it gets too quiet, I won't be able to sleep."

"'Cause you're used to it, right?" Georgia asks.

I just stare at her and don't say a word. Georgia is a smart girl, because she immediately knows that she just tried to play me. "I didn't mean to disrespect you," she says.

Both Darius and Carrie are staring at me as if I'm about to pop off at the mouth or something, so I just say in my very best voice, the one I use to impress my teachers, "I understand. Bushwick is an acquired taste. I'm surprised your family would want to move there."

Carrie chuckles. "Why are you suddenly talking like that?"

"Talking like what?" I ask.

"Darius, you noticed how she just changed the way she talked, right?"

"No," Darius says, shaking his head and looking dead at me. He's biting into his second chili dog now, and somehow he eats that sloppy food like it's gourmet.

"Zuri, you don't have to pretend to be someone you're not. Just be yourself. Admissions counselors really like that. You know, keep it a hundred," Carrie says with that annoying high-pitched voice of hers.

I raise both my eyebrows at this girl. "Keep it a hundred?"

"Yeah, keep it real." She takes a sip from her soda.

I let it slide because this isn't Bushwick and I'm on vacation. Sort of. But still, I entertain her nonsense because I have a few minutes to kill before I have to get back to the station. "So, Carrie, what are you doing in D.C.?" I ask, not because I want her to like me, but because it was her man who invited me over here and she's eyeing me like I'm the one checking for him.

"Oh, just hanging out with Darius," she says, cocking her

head to the side and leaning against Darius a little bit.

But he gently shoves her away.

"Well, I think that's my cue. It was nice running into all of you. See you back in Bushwick." I grab my bag and start to slide out of the booth.

"Wait!" Darius says, as he finishes chewing his chili dog, wipes his mouth, then his hands, and looks up at me. "My father's from around here. Well, Maryland. Carrie's grandparents live down here, too. My grandparents live in Chevy Chase," Darius says. "We drove down to chill with Georgia for a few days, and I was thinking of driving back up tonight. When are you heading back to Brooklyn?"

Carrie stares at him as if he's just broken some unspoken rule.

"Driving back?" I say, wide-eyed. "By yourself?"

"Yeah, I'm eighteen," he says. "I have my license and I've been driving since I was sixteen."

"Not in Brooklyn, though," Georgia adds. "It's easier to learn in Martha's Vineyard."

"Do your parents have a car, Zuri?" Carrie butts in.

This time, I cock my head to the side. She's a smart girl too, because she reads my answer all over my face. "So that's how rich people get down? They let you drive on the highway between states when you're only eighteen? Y'all are lucky."

Both Darius and Georgia just stare at me with their

matching tight jaws. Carrie is smirking.

"It's not luck. It's a necessity," Darius says. "And practice for when I go to college next year. I'll have to drive myself to and from campus when I visit Bushwick. I'm applying to Georgetown."

"Yeah, me too. In a few years," Georgia adds. "Because, obvi!"

"Yeah, obvi," I say, while nodding slowly. "You all are really from a different planet."

"No, we're not," Darius says. "In fact, now we're from the same block. I can drive you back to Brooklyn. I've done it plenty of times. But we should head out now before it gets too late, 'cause I have to drop Georgia off and get my stuff."

He doesn't wait to hear what I say. He doesn't even check in with Carrie, who's sitting there with her mouth open as if she can't believe what just went down. Darius is out of the booth already with his tray. He dumps his paper plate into the trash and starts heading out of the restaurant without looking back.

"Wait a second," Carrie says, grabbing her purse and running after him. "We were supposed to go back tomorrow. Why are you rushing, D?"

Darius pauses at the door, a surprised look on his face. "I thought you'd already booked a train ticket home. You complained about how carsick you were the whole way down."

"I didn't actually buy it!" Carrie says, pushing past him and out onto the sidewalk. Georgia and I quickly follow.

"Hold up," I interrupt. "I didn't agree to drive home with you just yet." Although if I do catch a ride home with Darius, Janae can get a refund for the bus ticket.

"You know what, forget it," Carrie says. "I'll figure something else out." She pulls out her phone and starts texting. "Whitney and Sam are going to Dodge City tonight anyway. I can hang with them."

Darius doesn't even try to stop her. "Cool, tell them I say hi," he says.

"Tell them yourself," Carrie replies, her voice icy cold. "I'm gonna get a cab." She flips her hair again and shakes her little narrow behind as she walks away.

I laugh under my breath.

Darius steps closer to me, putting his hands in his jean pockets. "Zuri, really. I can take you home. I'm a good driver—don't listen to Carrie." His voice is low.

"He really is!" Georgia chimes in.

I look up at Darius, then down at my phone, and see that I'm now running late for my bus. If I say no to Darius and then miss my ride, my parents will never let me out of the house again. I can say goodbye to Howard forever.

"I mean, I guess," I say, slowly. "But I get to deejay."

"Deal," Darius says, and his smile is wider than I've ever seen it. My stomach drops and I realize what I just agreed to. Four hours alone, in a car, with Darius Darcy. What would

Warren say to that?

A cab pulls up to the curb and honks at Carrie.

Georgia runs over to give Carrie a hug goodbye, and Darius waves politely to her. "I'll text you," he calls out.

"Bye, Carrie!" I shout. "See you back in Brooklyn!" I wave extra hard while grinning wide.

We wait until Carrie is out of sight and then begin walking down U Street toward the car.

"Are they going out?" I ask Georgia quietly.

"Carrie? No way," she says. Then she calls out to Darius, who is a few steps ahead of us. "Hey, bro! Zuri thought Carrie was your girlfriend!"

"Not in a million years," he says.

And in that moment, something stirs deep in my belly. I'm not supposed to care. But part of me is relieved that Darius isn't into someone so shallow and insecure.

"Is that a smile on your face?" Georgia asks, and I realize this girl is growing on me. I could see us being friends. Maybe.

"Yeah, 'cause you're kinda cool, Georgia," I say. "I can't wait for you to meet my sisters."

"Oh my god!" she squeals. "I can't wait either. We'll have to hang out before I head back to boarding school."

"Boarding school?" I ask, just as Darius holds open the shiny black front passenger door for me. It's a nice car, and it's not the one I usually see parked in front of their house back in Bushwick, but I don't ask any questions. For some reason, the polite gesture makes me nervous. Darius closes the door gently.

"Yeah," Georgia says as she slides into the back seat. "And now you get to meet my grandmother!"

"Wait, what?" I say, turning to Darius as he gets into the driver's seat.

"Uh, yeah, did I forget to mention that?" Darius says, and gives me a shy smile. He starts the car.

"Your grandmother? Seriously?" Suddenly I'm not sure this free ride is worth it. I need to call my parents and tell them about the change of plans, but maybe there's still time for Darius to drive me to the bus, and I won't need to tell them anything.

"She's harmless! I promise," Georgia says. "I've been living with her all summer."

"Really?" I ask with a raised eyebrow. I check the time and see that it's already almost seven. It's too late.

"Yeah, harmless," Darius promises.

"That's what I'm worried about," I mumble. But I click my seat belt closed.

As we drive out to the D.C. suburbs, I'm still stuck on the fact that I'm sitting in the front seat of a car that belongs to a boy I can't stand. And we're headed to his grandmother's house, of all places. Plus he's driving me two hundred miles back home. So I'm basically trusting Darius with my life right now. And an hour ago, I didn't even want to look at his face.

SEVENTEEN

THE BIG HOUSES here in Chevy Chase, Maryland, are pushed back away from the street, if you can even call it a street. It's more like a perfectly paved path to any- and everywhere. There are no potholes, no bumps, no double-parked cars—hardly any cars. Just wide-open smooth, curving road. And Darius drives as if he owns that path; as if this whole ride is his life and things are just as easy for him as this road.

I try not to let him see me checking out how he holds the steering wheel with one hand, how he leans back in his seat with all the confidence in the world, even though he's had his license for only two years. But he catches me looking at him, and I turn back to the car's window.

"You like lobster, Zuri?" Georgia asks from the back seat.

She's been asking me a billion questions about food, clothes, music, and places. Most of the things she brings up I've never heard of or experienced. So far, I know that they've gone skiing in somewhere called Aspen, go to somebody named Martha's Vineyard every summer (except for this one, because of the move), and how they are still hoping to take a trip to some place called the Maldives. And I can tell Georgia is not showing off or anything, she seriously thinks I know what she's talking about when she brings up these places.

"Sure," I say. It's a lie. I've been to Red Lobster, but never had the lobster because it's the most expensive thing on the menu, and with seven of us going out to eat for a graduation or a big birthday, no one is selfish enough to order lobster. I don't say this out loud, of course.

"Darius loves lobster. That's why Grandma is making it special for him," she continues. "And he has the nerve to eat two chili dogs before dinner. I swear he's her favorite, 'cause I asked for vegetarian lasagna yesterday, and she was like, no. But Darius gets lobster! Not even Ainsley gets that kind of treatment."

"Oh, so you're a grandma's boy?" I ask, side-eyeing him.

"Hardly. Georgia is exaggerating," Darius says as he pulls up to the biggest house I have ever seen.

If the Darcy house is a mini-mansion, then this house is a straight-up castle. There are tall white columns at the front entrance, and the windows are so wide that they might as well be walls. I try hard not to look as if I've never seen nice things before. I blink and look away from the house, down at my hands, my jeans, my book bag on the floor—anything to not look so sheltered.

The driveway curves around to the front of the house, and I keep it cool even as my phone keeps buzzing. It's seven thirty, and my bus left half an hour ago. My parents want to make sure that I'm on the bus, and my sisters are asking for pictures, especially of the cute boys on the Howard campus. I should snap one of Darius and send it to them. I have no idea how to tell my family that I'm not on the bus, that I'm with Darius, in his car, about to step into his grandmother's ginormous house. I would never hear the end of it.

Georgia jumps out of the car just as Darius shuts off the engine by pushing a button. He doesn't move from the front seat. I don't either.

"Are you sure you can get me home tonight?" I ask.

"I told you," he says, turning to me. "I got you."

I shift away when he says this. Back home, when we say we've "got somebody's back," we'll look out for them. But "I got you" is something else. It means that you're willing to fall back and know that the person will catch you. So I say, "You don't know me like that."

"What does that have to do with anything?" he asks.

169

"You said you got me. I don't know you well enough to trust you like that."

"You do trust me to take you home, right?"

"Home is a four-hour drive away. You just got your license. So I'm a little hesitant."

"I didn't just get my license. Okay. If you're still *hesitant*, I can drive the forty minutes back to Union Station for you to catch your bus," he says, checking his phone. "There'll be another one by nine o'clock tonight, so you'll be good. I just wish you would've made up your mind earlier."

"Hold up, you practically begged me to come here."

"I did not *beg* you. I asked. And you said yes. So why are changing your mind now? We're already here."

"Fine," I say, and open the car's door to step out into the clean, crisp air. I quickly slam it shut, just as a woman steps out of the house.

"Carrie? Is that you?" she says.

I freeze where I stand. Partly because she thinks I'm Carrie, even though we look nothing alike, and partly because she doesn't look like anybody's grandma.

This grandma walks toward the car wearing high heels, fitted dress pants, an apron, and hair so perfect that I'm sure it's a wig. And she almost looks younger than my own mother!

"Uh, Grandma, this is, uh . . . ," Darius starts to say as he comes out of the car.

"Oh, you're not Carrie," his grandmother interrupts,

stopping dead in her tracks and looking me up and down as if she's disappointed.

So I introduce myself, extending my hand out to shake hers. But she doesn't take it and instead turns to Darius.

"What happened to Carrie? I thought she was coming over for dinner." She sounds like the newscasters on TV—her words are perfect, her voice is the just the right tone of bougie, and her smile looks plastic. She walks up to Darius and plants a kiss on his cheek.

Darius steps back and looks away. His grandmother looks at me again.

I smile big and bright so she knows that my mama raised me right, and I try again. "I'm Zuri. Zuri Benitez," I say.

She cocks her head to the side as if my name isn't enough for her. So I wait for Darius to make the introduction she needs to hear. But it's Georgia who comes to my rescue.

"Zuri, this is our paternal grandmother, Mrs. Catherine Darcy. Grandma, she lives across the street from us in Bushwick!"

"And you dragged her all the way down here?" she says with her mascaraed and eye-shadowed eyes wide open.

"Dragged?" I say out loud. "Actually . . ."

"She was visiting Howard, and I . . . ," Darius starts to say.

"Howard?" Mrs. Darcy repeats.

"Yes. Howard," I say. "I'm sorry. I didn't mean to intrude. Where can I catch the nearest bus back to Union Station?"

"Zuri, no," Darius says. "Grandma, I invited Zuri 'cause she lives right across the street from our new house. I'm going to go back tonight, so I can give her a ride. We ran into her at Busboys and Poets."

"Oh, is that place still open?" Mrs. Darcy asks, and she just turns back around and walks into her big house with her heels clicking against the concrete.

If I thought the whole Darcy family was bougie, then this queen here is on a whole other level. I give Darius such a mean mug that he has to apologize with his whole body. He shrugs and gives me puppy eyes.

But again, Georgia is the first to actually say sorry. "Zuri, don't let our grandmother scare you. Once you get to know her, she's really nice."

And with that, I'm walking in front of Darius toward the other, bigger Darcy mansion, through their fancy door, and into what looks like a straight-up museum. I feel underdressed with my cheap sneakers and worn jeans. But still, as much money as they have, I decide that this grandmother of theirs is still shady. Money can't buy manners.

I don't look around. I don't admire all the fancy art on the walls. I don't stare too long at the framed photos or the shiny wooden furniture. I don't even sit down on the giant leather couch that wraps around the whole living room where a wide chandelier hangs from the middle of the high ceiling. I pull my book bag up over my shoulder and keep a straight face.

"So you just wanted to show off how rich your family is?" I ask Darius as he stands across the room messing with his phone. I ignore mine, 'cause I still have no idea what I'm going to tell my parents about not being on the bus by now.

He chuckles, puts his phone back into his pocket, and looks up at me. "There's still time to get back to the bus station if you want. I don't want to keep you here against your will, Zuri Benitez."

"Zuri. Just Zuri, Darius Darcy." I walk around the room, looking out the wide front window at all the green grass and tall trees in this place. I sigh, tap my foot, stare at my nails, anything to show Darius that I'm not impressed. Then I say, "I'm not some basic chick from the hood who thinks all that glitters is gold. I watch TV. I've seen fancy things before."

"These are not fancy things," he says. "These are . . . my grandparents' things. And my family has worked hard for them. I didn't bring you here to show off. I'm driving back to New York after dinner, and I wouldn't mind some company. In fact, I wouldn't mind *your* company."

Before I can think of a comeback, his grandmother's heels come clicking down the long hallway. "Darius, aren't you going to help me set up?" she asks before she even makes it into the living room, or whatever this giant room is called.

"I was just keeping Zuri company."

"Oh, you can wait here in the parlor, uh . . . how is it that you pronounce your name, darling?"

"Zuri. Zoo. Ri."

She fixes her mouth as if she's bitten into a lemon. "Oh, that's nice. Darling, I'm gonna steal my grandson for a bit. The washroom is just down the hall."

"I'm sorry. The what?"

"Washroom," she says. Then she shakes her head. "The bathroom. Wash your hands before dinner, sweetheart." She changes her voice with those last few words, as if she has a little bit of old-school hood hidden behind that hard face of hers.

Then she says, "Darius?" and walks away.

Darius motions for me to follow him out of the living room. I shake my head.

"Come on. She's just being my grandmother, that's all," he says.

"Not all grandmothers are that cold," I say.

"She's not cold, she's just . . . getting to know you, that's all. You're my guest. So it's fine."

And with that, I'm following him again, into a kitchen so white and bright, I have to blink a bunch of times just to be able to see straight. A long wooden table is next to the cabinets and shiny appliances. On it are white plates, wineglasses, white napkins, and sparkling silverware. Everything is set perfectly, looking like that farm-to-table restaurant Charlise works at. I almost want to take a picture of all this to send to her. She'd say all the wrong things—that I've hit the jackpot, that I need to get into this boy's pockets real quick, that I need to do something about that Carrie girl.

But I just keep cool, even after I see this washroom with two sinks and monogrammed towels. I stay in there for as long as I can, just staring at stuff and peeking into the cabinets. I don't even fix my messy fro in the mirror, splash some cool water on my face, or add any lip gloss. Until someone knocks.

"I don't keep my makeup in there," Georgia says when I finally open the door. "I could hook you up before you leave."

"I'm good" is all I say before sitting down at the table. I stare at a big red lobster on my plate, trying to figure out how to dig into it to get to the meat.

As dinner begins, Mrs. Darcy goes on and on about her foundation, where she helps women and children from impoverished countries with something called micro grants. Darius has to help with another thing called a gala. Georgia talks about her internship with some senator, and then Mrs. Darcy asks me questions. I'd felt invisible before then.

"Bushwick? I've lived there my whole life. And I intend to go back after college. It's the only home I know, and there's nowhere else in the world I'd rather be," I say, as cool as the cucumber salad on my plate.

"But Howard? It's a long way from Bushwick. And you sound like you've got a good head on your shoulders. Why not . . . Harvard or Georgetown? Darius will be applying this fall," Mrs. Darcy says. She's seated at the end of the table with Georgia on one side of her and Darius next to her. I'm sitting next to Georgia, but the table is so long that there might as well be two people sitting in between us.

"Well, I'd like to go to Howard because of its cultural legacy as a historically black college. I'm going to learn everything I can, and then I'm going back to my hood to help my people out." I leave the lobster alone and eat the linguine. I don't care how clumsy I look rolling the pasta onto my fork, because Mrs. Darcy doesn't seem to care about how disrespectful she's being to me.

"I'm sorry. Did you say your *hood*? So it is a little—how do I say—underdeveloped? Darius, I told your father to wait a few years, at least until Georgia is in college, to buy a house over there. You don't fit in. None of you do. Your parents did not raise you that way. I'm sure it's a culture clash for you, Darius. But my ambitious son wants to be a real-estate pioneer. I can't believe he's putting my dear grandchildren through all of that."

I pay attention to how she holds her fork with her pinky up, how she sips her wine, how she pats the side of her lips with the white napkin, and even how she looks down her nose at me.

I glance at Darius, who is shaking his head a little. He's not looking up at me at all. He doesn't say a word to come to my defense. And Georgia is too busy with her lobster to get a word in. So, like the girl from the *hood* that I am, I stick up for myself. "Bushwick is a very nice place to grow up, Mrs. Darcy.

We have block parties, we hang out on stoops together, and we look out for each other. And Georgia? Me and my sisters will look out for you when you come. Just like I look out for Darius now."

With that, he finally looks up, and I squint my eyes at him.

"Oh?" Mrs. Darcy says, and laughs a little while putting her fork down. "Is that why he brought you here? So you could *look out* for him?"

"Grandma!" Darius says.

Mrs. Darcy turns her whole body to Darius now and asks, "How did Carrie get home? I thought you two were hanging out in D.C. today. I was expecting her, and this is what you bring to my door instead?"

"Excuse you?" I say. "Mrs. Darcy, I didn't ask to come here. I'm supposed to be on a bus heading home right now. But your grandson invited me. So I will gladly invite myself *out*. Now, can someone please get me a cab?"

I stand from my seat, grab my bag from the floor, and start to make my way out of that kitchen.

"Oh, you will not talk to me like that in my own home, young lady," Mrs. Darcy says.

"And *you* will not to talk to *me* like that to my face."

"Grandma!" Darius says through clenched teeth. And that's all he says.

But I don't pay him any mind. I keep walking toward the living room, even as he comes chasing after me.

"I'm sorry, Zuri," he says. "Let me grab my things."

I open the front door and wait outside. I keep my arms crossed as my breaths get shorter, my heart races, and I feel like running back in there to curse that woman out one last time.

Georgia comes outside, and I look away from her.

"I'm sorry about that, Zuri."

"You're cool, Georgia, but your family is bougie as hell," I say.

"Please don't judge my family like that," another voice says. I turn toward the doorway to see Darius holding a small leather suitcase. "You wouldn't want me to call your whole family ghetto, now would you?"

Georgia's mouth falls open. Darius and I just stare at each other for a long second until his grandmother comes prancing to the door. That's my cue to keep walking away from that house.

"Darius, honey? It's getting dark. You should stay over and go home in the morning."

"I have to take Zuri home," he says.

"Well, you can take her back to Howard," she continues.

"I'll call you when I'm on the road, Grandma."

Darius comes around to the passenger side of the car to open the door for me.

"This whole thing was a mistake," I say as Darius gets into the car. "Please take me back to the bus station. And listen to your grandmother. You shouldn't drive all the way back to New York in the dark."

"I've done it before. And you shouldn't be on the bus by yourself."

"I'll be fine."

"Okay."

That's when I text my parents and finally tell them that I'll be catching a later bus home. Their responses are going to come flying through my phone, so I tuck it into my bag. I don't want to have to explain one more thing to them right now.

Darius starts the car as his grandmother stands in front of her house with her arms crossed. Georgia is waving to me frantically. I wave back.

"Your sister is cute," I say, just to let him know that there's at least one person in his family I like.

"Yeah, a little too cute and a little too naive," Darius says. He backs out of the driveway and has to put his arm around my seat and turn his body toward me to do so.

He leans in a little bit too much, and part of me thinks it's on purpose. When he's out of the driveway, he says, "Oh, sorry." Then he sighs as he drives away from his grandmother's house. "Thank you," he says.

"For what?" I say.

"For calling out my grandmother on her bullshit."

"I didn't mean to disrespect her, it's just that . . ."

"I know. You held your own."

I don't say anything to that. I just sit back in my seat, letting this strange day wrap around me like new clothes. It's familiar, but different, and makes me feel brand-new.

EIGHTEEN

"**WHAT DO YOU** like to listen to?" Darius finally asks after ten minutes of driving in silence down a highway. "You said you'd deejay, remember?"

"Trap," I lie. "Hood shit. Ratchet lyrics with the loudest bass."

"Okay," he says. "You'll have to be a little more specific."

"See? You should already know what I'm talking about when I say trap music. It should already be on your playlist. Now, what do you like to listen to?" I ask.

"Why don't you take a guess, since you already know me so well and what I *should* be listening to?"

"No. I don't like to play mind games."

"Really? You could've fooled me."

"What's that supposed to mean?"

"According to you, I should be doing all these things that'll make me more . . . what? Black? Did you write a manual or something?"

"Yes, I did. It's called *Boys in the Hood*."

"Ha. Ha. Very funny, Ms. Benitez."

"Ain't nobody laughing, Mr. Darcy. So, seriously. You don't got no trap music?" I ask, trying to figure out the buttons on his dashboard.

"You mean, do I have any trap music?" He says this slowly, enunciating every word.

"Hold up. Are you correcting me?"

"Yes."

I don't have any words for him. I just stare at the side of his face, and if he wasn't driving at sixty-five miles per hour down a highway right now, I'd mush him so hard, it would make him rethink his whole life.

But it's too quiet, so I reach for the radio at the same time he does, and our hands touch. I start to pull back, but he holds my hand for a moment as he stares out at the road. I slowly pull away.

"I need you to drive with both hands, Darius," I say as I notice the sign for Baltimore. "Wait, weren't you supposed to take me back to D.C.?"

He sighs. "Sorry. I wasn't thinking. I was so ready to head back to Brooklyn that I just hopped on ninety-five. We can go back, or you can catch a bus in Silver Spring. We're not too far from there."

I laugh a little. "You're trying to kidnap me?"

He doesn't laugh. "I would never do something like that." He's dead serious.

"Dang. Relax, Darius. I'm just joking. I can't wait to get back to Brooklyn either. So I'll ride with you." I want to take those last few words back, in case he reads too deep into them. But he doesn't respond.

I text my parents that there was a change of plans, that Darius is giving me a ride home. Mama doesn't even ask how or why or what. She just texts back a million heart emojis. I roll my eyes and shove my phone to the bottom of my bag. After a long, quiet minute, Darius says quietly, "You're probably hungry, since you barely ate any dinner. We can stop somewhere to get something to eat."

My first instinct is to say no. But I don't. My stomach twists. "Sure," I say.

I let the quiet swell between us for a moment. He never puts on any music and doesn't say another word. Neither do I. But the time is moving slowly, even though the car is zooming past miles and miles of trees and road. I sink into my leather seat and watch Darius because he can't watch me. He's more comfortable driving a car than I expected, using his turn signal to switch lanes and keeping his hands firmly on the steering wheel. Everything about him looks . . . confident. He knows who is. He knows this road. He knows this world. His skin looks extra smooth in the dim light of the setting sun. His face and whole body are relaxed. So I let my guard down a little bit. He glances at me for a quick second and shoots me a smile. This time, I don't look away. I keep watching him. Even though there's still some weird vibes between us, I feel safe.

Darius's ringing phone breaks the silence.

"Hey, Mom," he says as if he's talking to one of his friends.

"Darius?" his mother's voice is like music coming through the car's speakers. She almost sings. "Are you with that young lady from across the street?"

"Zuri? Yeah."

If my stomach was twisting before, then now it's a straight-up tornado.

"Well, her parents came to our door saying that she was with you. I assured them that you've made this trip several times and that she's in good hands. And I see you're on your way back to New York. Drive safe, honey!"

She hangs up before Darius explains anything. And I exhale a bit knowing that his parents are tracking his phone. He takes an exit off the highway, and I tense up because he's going a little too fast when he makes a sharp turn onto another road.

I dig out my phone and see that I have a new text from Warren and a ton from my sisters. I have no idea what to say to any of them right now. How could I possibly explain to Warren that I'm in the car with Darius?

We pull into the parking lot, and the lights of the rest stop flicker on in the gathering darkness. I open the door and get out of the car. Crickets chirp and the air is gentle. The hum of cars driving past is almost comforting. I know that we're near the highway, but this almost feels like the countryside or something, like I've been transported to a place I've only seen in movies.

We walk side by side and get hit by a blast of air conditioning when we step into the rest stop. Darius turns to me, concern etched between his thick eyebrows. "Wait. What do you like to eat?"

I look around at the fast-food options and walk ahead of him to a chicken spot. He follows. At the counter, I order the largest meal I can buy with my fourteen bucks. Darius orders fries and a club soda. While we're waiting, I realize that he's standing way too close behind me.

"Yo, ease up, bruh," I say with a smile on my face.

"I'm sorry," he says. "I thought you were cold. They're blasting the AC in here."

"Yeah right, Darius," I say, bumping my body against his. And he's right because it's hella cold in this fast-food restaurant and I notice the goose bumps on my bare arms.

"I can keep you warm while we wait," Darius offers innocently.

"What? No. I'm good. Really." I shake my head and turn away so he doesn't see me smile. Then I say, "I can keep *you* warm."

He hugs himself, rubs his arms, and goes, "Brrrr . . ."

I laugh. "Oh my goodness! You are so stupid!"

"Well," he says, holding out his arms. "I'm still cold."

I roll my eyes and shake my head just as they call our number for our order.

"That's all you're getting?" I ask.

"I just ate. And you barely touched your lobster."

"I'm not into lobster. And your grandmother spoiled my appetite."

"Zuri, I'm sorry about my grandmother," he apologizes again. "She can be a little uptight."

I just *hrumph*. I don't want to get into it again—and no amount of apologizing can fix that woman, anyway.

The cashier girl places our bags of food on the counter, and I reach into my pocket for my money. But Darius touches my arm, and he already has a card in his hand to pay for the food.

"I can pay for myself," I say.

"I knew you were going to say that. But really, it's my treat."

"Well, a'ight then." I can't help but give him a sliver of a smile as I let him pay.

I'm back at the car waiting for him to unlock the doors when I notice that he isn't behind me. He's sitting near a set of benches and tables in front of the restaurant. I didn't realize we were turning this into a full-on picnic.

I pause for a little bit to watch him open up the bags and pull out his food. He eats fries as if they're the most expensive thing in the world. He catches me looking at him and motions for me to come over.

For the first time during this whole trip, I'm able to sit back and take in the wide blue-orange sky and warm summer air. There are no tall buildings around or sirens or loud music and voices—just the soothing sound of speeding cars in the distance.

And Darius's brown eyes with those thick eyelashes, staring at me.

"Yes?" I ask as I dig into my two-piece meal. I don't feel any kind of way about eating fried chicken and fries in front of this boy, even as he refuses to look away.

"Nothing," he says, trying to hold in a laugh.

"You played yourself by only getting fries. You know you want some of this," I say with a mouthful of chicken.

"No, thank you. I'm just . . . amazed."

"You ain't never seen a girl eat fried chicken before?" I lick my fingers and take a sip of soda.

"No. Not like that."

"Of course not. I bet Carrie eats fried chicken with a knife and fork. Oh, wait. She's probably vegan."

"As a matter of fact, she claims to be."

"Figures."

"Why are you using her as a gauge? You're completely different, Zuri."

With that, he leaves me speechless for a hot minute. I finish my food, take a few more sips, and wipe my mouth. "I know

I'm different. That was my point."

"You're more than different. You're special, Zuri. I mean, damn. I've never met a girl like you." He looks down when he says this, as if he's been practicing or something, and he didn't know how I'd react.

I don't know what to say to that, even as my whole body tingles with tiny granules of sugar, as Madrina says. So I get up, wipe my mouth and hands with a napkin, toss the rest of my food into a nearby trash bin, and start heading back to his car. "We should hurry up. It's getting dark."

I'm almost near the car when I realize that he's not following me again. I turn around to see him standing a few feet away, just staring at me.

"Okay. You're creeping me out. For the record, my father knows I'm with you, he knows where your parents live, and he owns a machete," I say.

He smiles in a way I've never seen him smile before. I only shake my head and wait for him to open the car with his remote-control key thing. But instead he walks around to my side and is coming closer to me. I don't step back. I just stand there as he inches closer and closer, and before I know it, we're face-to-face. Still, I don't step back. Slowly, he leans in, breathing heavy, looking into my eyes, and his lips touch mine. He pauses as if making sure it's okay, and that's when I finish what he started. I fall into his kiss, making sure that I'm still in the lead, that I'm still in control, and he slips his hands around my waist and pulls me in. I pull him in even closer. We feel like one body.

And in that moment, I can't believe this is happening. This kiss, this hold, never crossed my mind as something that would be real. I hated him. I hated everything about him. But this, this isn't hate.

Finally he pulls away. But he looks into my eyes and raises his eyebrows as if asking me if I'm okay. I smile a little. He kisses me on the cheek before we make it back to the car. He opens the door for me and I silently slide into the seat. I reach over to open the door for him. "Thank you," he mouths. And every second of this moment is slowed down like dripping honey.

My stomach is in knots when we make our way back to the city. I push on the radio to fill the quiet, to hush my own spinning thoughts. Slowly Darius inches his hand across the armrest and weaves his fingers through mine. And I don't let go, even as my insides turn into gooey, sticky sweetness.

Haikus

I am that tall glass
of lemonade where sugar
sits at the bottom,

Never rising to
the top. Sweet and sour don't
mix to quench this thirst

Wrapping around my
throat where a bittersweet song is
lodged. You serenade

Me while I sip this
honey lemonade potion,
you are a love brew.

Damn boy, you got me
thirsty over you. Mouth dry,
lips chapped, I'm dreaming

Of quenching waters
and all I wanna do is
swim deep in this thing

Called lemonade where
bittersweet elixirs sooth
the soul like moist lips

Touching, bodies merged
in this dance while sugar stirs
to the top, whirling

Like Ochún in her
yellow dress swirling to the
drums, making all this

Sharp-tongued bitterness
submit to the queen bee called
my heart. You got me.

—*Thirsty*

NINETEEN

THERE'S SOMETHING HAPPENING to my body. But this isn't love. It was just a kiss.

Wasn't it?

I sit back in the car, feeling free. Darius is in full control, and I'm okay with it for now. We're easing toward New Jersey with music I've never heard before blasting in the car. Darius bops his head, sings some of the lyrics, licks his lips a few times, and glances at me plenty of times. I start to smile. My lips are a half moon, but my whole body is smiling too.

We're almost at the toll booths and the traffic comes to a crawl. Darius turns down the music and asks if I'm feeling okay.

I nod.

"Are you feeling better than you did earlier?" he asks again.

"What do you mean by 'better'?" I ask.

"Well, I know you weren't feeling my grandmother, or her house, or me."

"Oh, so you wanna know if I'm feeling better about *you*?"

He laughs. "Touché, Ms. Benitez. So how *do* you feel about me?"

I laugh too. "You don't waste any time, I see."

"I've already wasted too much time," he says, easing the car up close behind the one ahead of us.

"What do you mean by that?" I look directly at him this time because I want a direct answer.

"I should've kissed you a long time ago."

"Um, no, you should not have. I would've hated you even more."

"Oh, really? Hate is a strong word."

"And it's also a strong emotion."

"Emotions are feelings and feelings change. Is it safe to say that you don't hate me anymore?" He's now driving toward the E-ZPass lane, but the traffic is still slow.

That's not a question I'm ready to answer, not even for myself. And Darius knows this because I take too long to respond, so instead I ask, "Does your brother hate my sister?"

"Why would you think Ainsley hates your sister?"

"He broke up with her. Janae really liked him, and he dropped her like a sack of dirty laundry. So I see how you

Darcy boys do," I say, crossing my arms.

He laughs a little. "Ainsley didn't drop her. And we Darcy boys don't do anything. You're a little know-it-all, aren't you, Ms. Benitez?"

"I'm not a little anything, Mr. Darcy. And Ainsley dropped Janae. I saw the whole thing go down at that cocktail party of yours. Why did he break up with her just like that? Did he think he was too good for my sister?"

"No. He didn't think that at all," Darius says as he drives through the E-ZPass toll. The traffic starts to speed up, and I want to end the conversation now so that he can focus on the road. But he keeps talking. "Ainsley wouldn't do that. He just . . . when he falls for a girl, he falls hard."

"Okay. So clearly he didn't fall for Janae. But still, that was really shady. He played her right in his own house in front of all those people."

"Zuri, I told Ainsley to break it off with Janae."

I just look at him. And he keeps his eyes on the road. "What?"

He inhales, and the car sways a little bit. But he definitely needs to clarify that, so I ask again.

"Darius, what did you just say?"

"I told Ainsley that I didn't think Janae was good for him." He exhales. He switches to the right lane and slows down a little bit.

"Okay." I nod and purse my lips. "You told Ainsley that you didn't think Janae was good for him." I repeat every word he said, just to make sure I heard him correctly. This is the most I can do right now without calling him everything but a child of God, as Mama would say.

"Zuri, I was wrong. I know that now," he says. He keeps trying to look at me as he drives.

"Oh, you were dead wrong, Darius," I say really loud. I put my neck and hands into every word so he knows that I'm pissed. He's the only one who can hear and see me right now. And I'm that close to cursing him out too. "What? So *you* thought Janae wasn't good enough for your brother? You don't want no gold-diggin' hood rats up in his pockets? Well, guess what— I'm a hood rat too, and sorry to disappoint you, but I don't dig for gold. I dig for dreams, goals, and aspirations. And so does Janae. It was *his* loss, Darius. And yours too, for making such a dumb mistake and judging us like that!"

"Zuri, I know," he says, raising his voice too. "I didn't think . . ." He pauses. A car passes us and he speeds up a bit. "I didn't think I'd like you the way I do now."

"Excuse you?" I say, turning to looking at him again.

"I like you, Zuri Benitez. I was wrong about Janae. And you. I'd like to get to know you better. Let me take you out. Make it a legit date."

I can't help but laugh. It's either because what he just said is hella funny or I don't know how to respond and it makes me nervous. Or both. So I keep laughing.

"What's so funny?" he asks.

"You," I say. "You are funny, Darius Darcy."

"I wasn't joking, though."

"Yes, you were, because I can't believe you would ask me out after what you did to both my sister and Warren. In fact, we shouldn't've kissed at all. Now *that* was a mistake."

"So you think I'm a bad person?"

"Yes! You judged them, and you turned your nose up at them. And me. I know what this is, Darius. You're so used to girls throwing their panties at you that you're trying to figure out why I'm not doing that too. You think you can kiss me and have me wrapped around your little finger like Carrie. Nope! Find some other impressionable chick on the block, because I am not the one."

"I don't think like that, Zuri," he says quietly as he places both hands at the top of the steering wheel.

"You don't have to think like that, Darius. You already are that. I saw your game from across the street," I say, folding my arms and turning my whole body away from him.

After a few long minutes and a long drive down a whole other highway, he says, "Zuri, I'm sorry I can't be more like your *boy in the hood*, Warren."

"Oh, you can never be like Warren," I say way too loudly.

"I would never want to be like Warren. Not in a billion years," he says.

"I know you don't like him just 'cause he's from the projects and all. Me and Warren, we're made of the same stuff. If you can't stand him, then clearly you can't stand me."

"You know, Zuri. Sometimes I'm baffled by how judgmental you are," Darius says, taking one hand off the steering wheel.

I side-eye him. "Baffled? I should be the one who's baffled. And you, Darius Darcy, are the walking definition of judgmental."

"I'm not judgmental. I'm just an excellent judge of *character*. You fall short in that department."

"Character? So you judged my sister's *character*?"

"Yes, I did. And she's cool," he says. "If you need some tips on how to accurately judge a person's character, just let me know."

"Thanks, but no thanks. I know how to *read* people just fine."

Darius inhales and says, "So you *read* that boyfriend of yours and decided to ignore the writing on the wall."

"That boyfriend of mine? Warren? I don't judge a book by its cover."

He laughs a little. "So you've read a whole book called *Warren from the Projects* and you know everything about him."

"What does that even mean?"

"I think you need to stay away from Warren," he says flat out. We're in the left lane now, and he's driving slower than before.

So I laugh. "Of course you would say that."

"You don't know Warren like I do, Zuri."

"You're right. I don't. I know the real him."

"You know what? Fine. Have it your way." Darius raises the volume on the music, and this is what takes up the widening silence between us. Every now and then, the recent memory of that kiss tries to creep into my thoughts, but I shut it down. I was fooled by my own emotions, by the distance from home. And as the lights of Manhattan appear on the horizon, it's like everything I knew about Darius comes right back to slap me in the face.

TWENTY

BOTH MAMA AND Papi are waiting up for me when I get back home. It's a little past midnight, and that was the longest car ride of my life. We hit some traffic as we got into the city, and Darius was playing the most boring music ever. I've never been happier to see my block.

"Are you okay, mija?" Papi asks as he gets up from the couch to examine my face and kiss me on the forehead.

"Yeah, I'm fine," I say groggily. I'm bone tired, and I really don't want to answer any of his questions right now.

"So are you two seeing each other?" Mama says.

"Ma!" I say. "Are you serious? Good night!"

I make my way to the closed door of our bedroom. I can hear my sisters giggling even with the lights turned off.

"Darius and Zuri sittin' in a tree" is the very first thing I hear when I open the door.

"What are you, like, five? Shut up, Layla!" I say as I turn on the lights.

"K-I-S-S-I-N-G," Kayla finishes off.

"First comes love," Layla adds.

"Then comes nothing!" I cut her off. "There was no kissing, there's no love, there's nothing. Now shut up and go to sleep!"

"Are you boyfriend and girlfriend now?" Layla asks anyway.

"No!" I almost yell.

"You think he likes you?" Kayla asks, sliding down out of her bed to sit cross-legged on the floor, as if I'm about to tell them a bedtime story.

"No. He hates me and I hate him. And that's the end of that. I don't wanna talk about those stupid boys. Why don't you ask me about Howard instead?"

"Okay," Layla says. "So did you see a lot of fine boys at Howard?"

"Oh, come on, Layla!"

"Is his grandmother's house even bigger than the one across the street?" Marisol asks.

"Yes, and she's even snootier than those boys across the street. And their parents. She's the worst!" I say as I climb out of my clothes. I can't help but notice the smell of Darius's car on my shirt.

"Was that his car? And is he making payments, or is it leased?" Marisol asks.

"I don't care!"

"Then what did y'all talk about for four hours, though?" Janae finally asks. But I know deep down inside she's curious about something else.

"School, college, stuff," I lie.

I shut out my sisters' voices as they keep giggling and guessing at what we talked about.

When I'm finally in bed and the lights are turned off again, Janae slides in with me. I scoot over, knowing exactly why she's here. She won't sleep until she finds out. So I speak first.

"No, I didn't see Ainsley," I say. "But Howard was lit!"

She wraps me in a hug, and she slides back out of my bed. I wish I could make Janae hate Ainsley as much as I hate Darius.

The next afternoon, while my sisters are out of the room and it's just me and my notebook, I notice a missed text from Warren last night. I text back a quick *Hey* before I start typing a long response. Another text comes in with a simple *Hey*. I immediately notice that it's not from Warren after all. It's from a number I had called earlier, and immediately my insides twist.

It's Darius. I don't know how to respond, but before I even think of something, my phone rings.

"Hello?" I say nervously.

"Can you come outside?" Darius asks, with his voice sounding much deeper than in person.

At the same moment, another call comes in. It's Warren. I tell Darius to hold.

"What up, Z?" Warren sounds way too cheerful for so early in the morning. "I'm working out over here at the Irving Square playground. You good to shoot some ball?"

I laugh. "Yeah, that'll be cool. Just hold on a minute. I gotta get rid of somebody."

I switch over to Darius. "I can't. I gotta meet Warren in a few," I say without hesitation.

"Warren?" I can feel him bristle. "That's actually what I wanted to talk to you about. You caught me off guard last night, but Warr—"

"You know what, I really don't want to hear it. I'm good. I'll see you around the way, Darius. And thanks for getting me home safe."

With that, I switch over to Warren and tell him to meet me out front in a few minutes. I can't wait to see him and tell him about Howard.

The minute I step outside my door, Warren shows up on my stoop with that smooth smile of his. But even as I sit, listening to Warren crack jokes about the guys on the courts and other people we know from around our way, I can feel something tugging at me across the street. It's a soft pull, like someone touching the bottom of my shirt, or a light tap on my shoulder.

I glance up at one of the Darcy house windows, and I spot Darius looking at us. I quickly look away. Warren has his back to the house, and while he checks his phone, I look back up at the window. I stare at Darius for a moment, and he stares back.

"Zuri Benitez," Warren says. "I wanted to see you again."

At the same moment a text comes through my phone. It's Darius, again.

Then *another* text comes in. "What does he want?" I say out loud.

Warren glances at the windows across the street.

"He wants you, Zuri," Warren says with a smirk. "Just ignore him."

My phone keeps buzzing, and I watch Darius type quickly. I can't ignore him, because his texts keep flooding my phone.

I'm sorry

But I really need to tell you something

Warren isn't a stand-up guy

I would never lie to you

Please believe me

"Why don't you just tell him to come over here," Warren says, and I almost jump. He's trying to look over my shoulder, and I shift away.

Believe you about what? I respond. *Just tell me what's going on.*

I watch Darius pause and read my texts. It's like I can see his jaw tighten from across the street. Then he begins typing again.

Gigi is in boarding school because Warren took sexy pictures of her
He sent them to his friends
"What the fuck?" I gasp.
Then they got around to the whole school
That's why she's staying with our grandmother
He fucked up her reputation
But please keep this a secret
I really don't want anyone to know

I look up over at Darius, and our eyes lock. I try to process all this information about Warren, the boy who's sitting right next to me. Has Warren been lying about everything? Is this the reason he almost got expelled? I can't believe it. But then I think about Georgia. She's mad sweet. Photos getting around isn't something you just make up. My stomach stirs. If anything like that happened to one of my sisters . . . I can't even finish the thought. I'd hate Warren too, if I was Darius.

I see him typing. The three dots hover.
Zuri? he writes.
I pause.
I promise not to tell, I write back.
"Yo, Zuri. What. Is. Going. On?" Warren says.

I turn toward him, but I can barely look him in the face. My blood is boiling.

"Is it true?" I ask Warren point-blank. I narrow my eyes at him.

"Zuri, is what true? What just happened?"

"What you did to Darius's sister."

"Damn, is that what he just told you? Seriously, I can explain."

I get up from the stoop and start pacing, my mind buzzing. "The only thing you need to explain is how you were nasty enough to take pics of a fifteen-year-old girl. What the fuck, Warren?"

"So it's like that, huh?" He gets up too. He's a step above me, and now he towers over me. But I refuse to be intimidated.

"Get the fuck outta my face, Warren!"

Warren glares at me, but he does what I say. The gate slams shut behind him, and he walks down the street without looking back. I feel all the air leave my body, and it seems like my heart is screwed on backward. I went from catching feelings for Warren to cursing him out in the span of a minute.

I look up and see Darius is still standing in the window. He nods at me, once. I bite my lip as I nod back. Darius steps away from the window. I sink down onto the steps and cover my head in my hands.

"What's going on?" Janae calls out from upstairs.

My sisters are watching from the bedroom window. Madrina's curtains are open. And maybe the whole block had their eyes on me, Warren, and Darius.

And that's when I know for sure that those boys moving onto this block has changed everything.

TWENTY-ONE

WHEN I REACH Madrina's door, it's already slightly open. I can see her colorful walls covered in bright artwork: fake Picassos, African masks, Caribbean art, and even the stuff my sisters and I made in grade school, framed and placed beside all the other eclectic knickknacks Madrina has around her home. It was Madrina who gave me my first poetry journal, who encouraged me to write down everything I saw.

"Madrina!" I call out, and my voice echoes. I need to talk to Madrina about this boy. That kiss. Those photos. And this thing I can't quite describe that's swimming deep inside me.

I search the kitchen, the bathroom, and finally I hear a faint voice coming from behind the closed door of her bedroom. I knock first. Then I open the door to find Madrina lying in her bed.

"Madrina, what's wrong?" I ask. I rarely come into her bedroom because never, ever have I seen her laid up in bed in the middle of the afternoon.

The lump beneath the blankets shifts, and she mumbles something.

"Madrina?" I take slow steps toward her bed.

She pulls back her covers, and for the very first time in my whole entire life, I'm seeing my madrina without any makeup. She's a little darker and her face looks smaller. The wrinkles on her forehead are like ocean waves, her eyes are deeper and piercing, and her thin lips stretch into a weak smile when she sees me.

"Zuri? Cómo 'tás?" she says. Her voice is still deep and booming, but it comes from a shallow place now.

"Why are you in bed?"

"Because I'm resting," she says, and turns over to her side to face me.

"No riddles, Madrina. Tell me straight up. What's going on?" I crouch down beside her bed so that we're eye to eye.

"You're so bossy, you know. The bossiest of all your sisters," she says, smiling.

"I get it from you, Madrina. Where's Colin?" I take her hand and squeeze it. It's cool, smooth, and dry.

She squeezes my hand back. "Zuri. You're also hardheaded.

You have all these walls around you that it's like your heart is locked up in some room."

I pull away from her. "You want me to get you some water? Did you have something to eat yet?" I'm too worried about Madrina to even tell her about what happened with Darius on the drive from D.C.

She starts to get up from beneath the covers. She's wearing a flowery nightgown, and for the first time, I suddenly see how thin she's gotten. She's still a little chunky and soft, but it's different. For the first time ever, she looks frail. She opens a drawer in her nightstand, pulls out a fifty-dollar bill, and slides it over to me.

"Keep the change," she says, and gets up from her bed.

I take the fifty dollars from her with no questions asked. And no answers, either. I watch her for a long minute as she struggles to pour the boiling water from an electric kettle on her nightstand into a mug. Her hand is shaking like I've never seen it before. I quickly get up to help her, but she shoos me away.

"I had this nice soup called el bisqué at that new farm restaurant. Go get me that el bisqué, Zuri! It was so delicious," she says.

Slowly I walk out of her apartment, feeling as if I should still be in there with her. And hoping that when I come back, she'll be all dressed, with her head wrapped and beads and makeup and deep, joyous laughter.

* * *

"I kept trying to get her to order something else, but she kept asking for more bowls of the bisque," Charlise says as she goes through a stack of paper menus. "And I kept saying, 'Madrina, it's bisque, not el bisqué. The E is silent.' She spent like two hundred dollars all by herself."

The menus are printed on thick, textured paper with fancy gold lettering. I keep staring at the name of this place, Bushwick Farm. It's not on any sign outside the building. The people who need to know that this is a farm-to-table restaurant already know it's a farm-to-table restaurant. Charlise says that farm-to-table means that the chicken is supposed to still be clucking when it's on your plate and the vegetables taste like wet soil. The food is *that* fresh. The people who come here to eat mostly are white, mostly are rich, and mostly ignore us as if we're ghosts.

That's how they treat Charlise as they come into the restaurant. She's supposed to check to see if they have a reservation, seat them, and hand them their menus. But most of them just walk past her as if she's not even there. Good. She won't get in trouble for talking to her friend while she's supposed to be working.

"She was here by herself? Not even with Colin. Why?" I ask her.

"Madrina said she's souping it all up before the gringos take over," Charlise says. "And speaking of soup, which one did she want? The fire-roasted tomato or the lobster one?"

"She didn't ask for soup, she asked for el bisqué. I mean, bisque."

"Bisque *is* soup, DAH-ling!" Charlise raises an eyebrow and holds her pinky up, and I laugh. "You better learn to say them fancy words. You're gonna be out in the world soon, college girl. And besides, rich boy from across the street knows how to say it."

A chill runs up my spine. I quickly look away from her so that she doesn't see my face. She would probably know everything just by looking into my eyes. A few customers walk in, distracting Charlise. She grabs a couple of menus and walks them outside, where they ask to be seated.

In the evenings, they block off a section of the sidewalk and put out wooden folding chairs, tables covered with white cloth, fancy plates, and wineglasses. That whole setup always looks strange to me, because this place used to be an auto-repair shop when I was little. It was closed for a couple of years, and then out of nowhere, it seemed, it became a fancy restaurant. I bet these people don't even know that car exhaust and engine oil once filled this place. I force myself to think about all these things so Charlise can't tell that somewhere in the back of my mind is the thought of Darius and our drive from D.C. together.

211

"So. When was rich boy in here?" I ask.

"About a week ago, with his whole family. At the same time as Madrina, in fact. She was eyeing them the whole time. Then rich boy came over and said hi. Introduced himself and everything."

"Really? Wait. Which rich boy?" I ask.

"The fine one!" She tries to hold in a laugh.

I give her a look. Then she bursts out laughing, and the bartender looks over at us. He just smiles and shakes his head.

"Okay, it was Ainsley. And they were all nice to me. Too bad Janae is not going out with him anymore. How's Warren, by the way?"

I shrug. "We're done."

"Wait. What?"

"It's complicated" is all I can manage to say. I want to keep Darius's secret. And Georgia's.

"Well, I have some news." She tries to hide her smile.

"What is it, Charlise?"

She grins wide, revealing all her teeth, as if what she's about to tell me will shock me.

"Or, *who* is it?" I grab my phone to check if I missed a photo on Charlise's instagram.

"Wait, Zuri," she says. "He's about to come in."

I look out the opened glass door to the restaurant and count down. Ten, nine, eight . . . and in walks Colin, with that fake limp of his, and that cheesy grin as if he thinks he's

God's gift to girls. As soon as he's close enough to where I'm sitting, I say, "Hey, Colin. Madrina already sent me here for her el bisqué."

"Oh, that's cool. You should try some of that bisque too, Z. It's dope."

And right before my eyes, he reaches over the podium in front of Charlise and kisses her on the lips. I throw my hands up. "Oh, hell no!"

"See? I told you she'd get all in her feelings," Colin says.

I take a deep breath and stare at the two lovebirds for a minute. I want to be a supportive friend. I don't want to seem like a hater. "You know what, Colin? I'm happy for you two. Really."

Charlise's face lights up and she smiles bright. "Thank you, Zuri!" Then she turns to Colin. "See? I told you she'd be all right with this."

Colin wraps his arm around Charlise's neck, pulls her in, and plants a big fat kiss on her forehead, just as a well-dressed couple walks in. I step aside and watch Charlise shoo Colin away, then attend to the guests. It's a long minute before I realize that the couple is none other than the Darcy boys' parents, and I want to run out of there. But Charlise points to me, and they both turn. Darcy dad smiles. Darcy mom doesn't. Then she smiles a fake smile.

I grab the paper bag with Madrina's bisque and quickly leave that place, walking really fast down Knickerbocker Avenue and back to my building. As my heart races, I think that maybe I read the Darcys wrong. Maybe the Darcy mom has a bad case of resting bitch face. Maybe they were just in an argument and they went to that restaurant to patch things up. But then again, first impressions are everything. Madrina says to trust my gut. My gut told me that the Darcys were all conceited, and their sons thought that they were better than us. But I kissed one of them. And he apologized to me. Sort of.

As I'm walking back to my building, I get a text from Darius.

Hey, he types again.

I take a breath.

Hey, I respond.

TWENTY-TWO

Him: *Zuri, I'm sorry about everything.*

Me: . . .

Him: *Sorry about Warren too. I know you liked him.*

Me: *Don't apologize for Warren. He's an asshole. You proved your point.*

Him: *I wasn't trying to prove anything.*

Me: . . .

Him: *You and him still a thing?*

Me: *We're nothing. You did see me curse him out, didn't you?*

Him: *I couldn't miss it. It was epic.*

Me: . . .

Him: *Can we have a do-over?*

Me: . . .

Him: *Please, Zuri Luz Benitez. ZZ.*

Me: . . .

Him: *???*

Me: *I'll give you another chance. But you best step up your game.*

Him: ☺☺☺

Madrina left her apartment door unlocked for me.

"Madrina!" I call out as I'm staring at Darius's texts. "I got your soup! And it's *bisque*, not el bisqué. It's a fancy word for soup."

She doesn't say anything and I look up from my phone and towards her bedroom. "Madrina?"

"I heard you, mi amor," she says with an unusually raspy voice. "Just put it down, okay? Gracias, mija."

She coughs a couple of times as I start to reply to Darius's last text. But I don't send anything. I walk out of Madrina's apartment with my head in a shimmery pink fog. I read Darius's texts over and over again as I climb the steps, almost tripping.

TWENTY-THREE

AGAIN, I'M LYING to my parents and my sisters about being with a boy. I can't believe I've become *that* girl.

Charlise is covering for me. We're supposed to be going to the movies. My sisters side-eye me because they know I don't like movies. I explain that it's Charlise's last summer before college and they buy it. They think I'm going to meet boys at the theater, and I don't argue with them. It's better than letting them know that I'm meeting the boy across the street who I'm supposed to hate right now.

I feel bad about not telling Janae, though.

I told Darius to meet me at the L train stop and to leave home before me. There's no way he can come pick me up at my door.

He texts me that he's almost at Wyckoff Avenue. I'm two blocks behind him, and I speed up a bit. Even though I've agreed to hang out with him, I'm not really sure what I'm getting into. A ride home from D.C. was one thing, but Darius Darcy taking me out on a date is another.

I don't see him when I get to the train station. He hasn't texted his exact location. So I look around, and two minutes go by. I'm a little conscious of what I'm wearing—a loose-fitting sundress and sneakers. I tried to be cute, but not too cute, so he doesn't think that I'm trying too hard. My stomach stirs a little bit, thinking that he might be playing me or has stood me up, or something. A small part of me still doesn't trust him.

Suddenly I feel someone's presence behind me, so I quickly elbow them in the belly. I turn around to see Darius doubled over, holding his stomach.

"You can't be rolling up on nobody like that on the subway!" I say.

"Tell him, sis!" someone nearby calls out.

And I laugh.

"I was trying to surprise you," Darius says in a strained voice.

"Nope. Not here. And not with me. This isn't Park Slope," I say.

And he laughs. His laugh softens me a little bit. And I return his hug. He wraps both his arms around my upper body while I wrap mine around his waist. His body is strong and I almost stay there for a second too long, but then I remember where I am.

I'm still in my hood, and somebody might see us and tell my parents.

On the train, the first thing I say is "This isn't a date." I said this to Warren too.

"I know," he says, shrugging. "You can call it whatever you want. Bottom line is that we're doing this, whatever this is."

There's not much I can say to that. So I just nod. "You're saying all the right things. Did you practice or something?"

He laughs. "Or something. Let's just say I have an idea of what pisses you off."

"So you're trying to avoid those things?"

"Basically."

"That's not very authentic."

"Well, I'm just trying to be on my best behavior and be a gentleman."

"There you go with those good manners of yours," I say. The train inches toward Morgan Avenue, and I notice how the people who started getting on at the last few stops look different than the people who were on this train when we got on.

"What's wrong?" Darius asks. He slides away from me a little bit and turns his body toward me, as if I'm about to give him the most interesting answer ever.

I see him now. For the first time since knowing him, I see

him. He still dresses as if he's off to a teaching job or something. But his jawline is not as tight. And his eyes are smiling. He looks as if he sees me too. So I open up to him. "I've been taking this train my whole life. The train is the same. The stops are the same. But the people are different."

He looks around. "I know what you mean."

"Do you really, though?"

"Yes," he says, and moves closer to me again. "But I don't want to talk about that now, because I'd rather hear about the last book you read."

"If I tell, then we'll have to talk about that," I say.

He smiles. "Okay. What's your favorite food?"

Again, this is something that no one has ever asked me. It's a simple question. So I let everything about this moment be simple. And he hangs on to my every word.

The rest of the afternoon goes by like a warm summer breeze. We get off at Bedford Avenue on the L train, and even though I rep Brooklyn all day, every day, I still never have been to Williamsburg. The streets here are narrow and filled with artsy white people with tattoos, piercings, thick beards, and colorful hair. There's nothing but little shops and restaurants on this strip of Bedford Avenue. I eat gourmet pizza with him. I sip bubble tea and have frozen yogurt. He insists on paying, even though this is not a date. I walk into my very first vintage store, like the ones Janae described up near her college in Syracuse.

"You want it? I can buy it for you," Darius says as I hold a sweatshirt up to my body.

"I know you can buy me anything I want. The question is, do I want you to buy me anything?" I say, putting the sweatshirt back on the rack.

I'm about to move to another rack when I feel Darius tug at my dress. I stop as he gently pulls me toward him. He takes both my hands in his hands. I step closer to him until our bodies touch. Out of the corner of my eye, I spot our reflection on a fitting-room mirror. I turn to see just how perfect we look together. He's way more put together than I am. His clothes are newer, more expensive. I look cute, but still a little hood, a little less polished. He watches us too. And he slips his arms around my waist while still looking at us. I lean in to his chest.

"Perfect," he whispers.

His breath reaches the back of my neck, and my whole body tingles. So I face him again and reach up to kiss him. We kiss right there in the middle of the vintage store, in front of a fitting-room mirror, for all these hipsters to see.

Someone says, "Awww!"

Still, we don't stop. And I melt. Darius hugs me so tight, picking me up off my feet, it feels as if he's inhaling me. And I'm exhaling him.

When we finally release each other, he still holds me in his arms, trying to smooth back my fro.

"Save your energy. My hair doesn't move," I say, just to break up that heated moment.

He laughs and I pick up the sweatshirt—a logo of Hillman College from that old TV show *A Different World*—and hand it to him. I walk out of the store and wait for him outside as he pulls out his wallet with a big fat smile on his face.

For the rest of our date, we don't stop holding hands. We talk about music, his school, my school, and soon our little block in Bushwick extends all the way out to here too. Everything about this afternoon with Darius Darcy feels like home.

I never knew that deep kisses, hand-holding, and small talk could last for so long, because by the time we get back on the L train and get off on Halsey Street, we've talked about everything under the sun. We forget that we aren't supposed to be seen together until we get to the corner of our block. Still, we don't move away from each other. I have a big smile on my face, and so does Darius as we get to my door.

"It was nice getting to know you, Zuri Benitez," he says as he stands in front of my stoop.

"Likewise, Darius Darcy," I reply.

He eases his hand against the side of my neck, and I lean my head into it, kissing his wrist. I close my eyes for a little bit and feel this whole thing, this sweet thing, take over my whole soul. It's something I feel in my bones. No. Deeper than bones.

When I open my eyes, I can tell from Darius's face that he feels it too. His eyes are in another place, even though they're staring right at me. His smile is so soft that it looks like it's in a deep, deep rest. Finally he kisses me one last time for the day. And I don't care one bit who sees us.

In fact, I want my family, my block, and my whole hood to see us.

TWENTY-FOUR

NOT EVEN A week goes by before Darius asks to see me again. But this time, he insists that it's a date.

"Come with me to Carrie's party," he says when I run into him at Hernando's. Well, we kind of, sort of, planned to run into each other. At about eight in the morning, he texted me that he was going for a run with Ainsley and that he was picking up two bottles of Gatorade beforehand. I volunteered to get Papi a tin of Bustelo coffee when I spotted Darius walking out of his house.

Darius already has on his workout clothes—a fitted T-shirt, basketball shorts, and sports leggings or whatever they are. I'm in my drawstring not-pajama pants and a T-shirt, and my fro is in thick braids. We're standing in the middle of the aisle, away from Hernando's nosy eyes, but his cat, Tomijeri, eases his fat, furry body between both our legs, eavesdropping.

"Carrie? You know I don't like her, right? And she doesn't like me," I say as I hold Mama's EBT card in my fist. I really don't want to pull it out in front of Darius.

"You really shouldn't care about that," he says with a smile.

I have to cast my eyes down when he smiles.

His knuckles softly graze the side of my face, and immediately my whole body melts.

"I like you a lot, Zuri Benitez," he whispers.

I smile. "Then you got my back if something goes down between me and Carrie, right?"

He laughs. "You'll fight over me? I didn't think you were that type of girl."

I laugh too. "I didn't say I'd be fighting over you. I'm only throwing jabs if she come at me with some nonsense."

"Okay, but don't underestimate bougie rage. That's on another level."

"Zuri-looose!" Hernando calls out when we reach the counter. "Those Benitez women . . . you better watch out!" he says to Darius.

Darius and I walk out of the bodega like two old friends, or new friends. Or something else, something better and different.

My sisters and Madrina can read the *different* all over my face and body. So this time, I tell my family the truth—that I'm going on a date with Darius Darcy.

"Janae, you're acting like I just won the lotto!" I say to my sister. She's picking out clothes for me to wear when I meet Darius. But everything she puts out, I put away. She wants me to borrow her heels. But I'm a sneakers girl. So we compromise. I settle on a short dress with sneakers, and I rock my bamboo earrings.

She watches me get dressed, fixing and fussing over me. "Zuri. Just have a good time, okay? Darius is really nice. Whatever you thought of him before, he proved you wrong, right?"

"You okay, sis?" I ask, smiling, only because she's smiling. But her eyes are not smiling.

"Yeah," she says, furrowing her brows. "Why wouldn't I be?"

"Janae?"

"Z, I'm over Ainsley. Trust me."

"Like, you're not even wondering what he's doing right now?"

"No, Zuri. I'm good. Really," my big sister says. But I know her too well. I see it in her face as she glances at the top-floor windows of the Darcy house.

Mama bursts into our room clasping her hands, with a giant smile on her face. "I'm so happy for you!" she sings.

"Oh, come on!" I say, rolling my eyes so hard I give myself a headache. This is the last thing I wanted to happen. For Mama, me having a cute and rich boyfriend who comes from a good family is right up there with getting a scholarship to college.

When I'm dressed and ready to leave, Papi only looks up from his book and grunts. But when I catch his eye again, he gives me a half smile and a nod. This is our secret understanding. This is okay with him. Just okay. He approves for now, but he wants to make sure that I'm happy. If I am, then he is. I smile at him.

"Bueno," he mouths.

Even though I look extra cute with my outfit and my hair done up in the biggest fro possible, Darius is two steps ahead of me. He's actually wearing a tight-fitting leather motorcycle jacket. He has on shoes with no socks so I can see his ankles, and he smells way too good. I do my best to keep my cool on the cab ride to Park Slope, where Carrie lives, but tingles go up my arm when Darius takes my hand and holds it in his the entire time.

"Don't be nervous," he says.

"Who said I was nervous?" I ask. But he just gives my hand a squeeze. I wonder what there is to be nervous about.

The moon is round and full tonight, and it casts a dim light on this neighborhood where the whole block is lined with tall trees and brownstones. This is a part of Brooklyn that gets shown on TV.

There's a small crowd of teenagers standing outside one of the brownstones. The cab pulls up to the curb; Darius pays the driver and comes out first. As soon as his no-sock-having foot steps onto the sidewalk, these kids gather around him like he's the coolest person they've ever met. I'm left standing by myself as the cab drives away. So I start to make my way around the group and go up the steps leading to the brownstone's open front door.

"Zuri, this is everybody," he says, pointing to everyone who's standing around him. "Everybody, this is Zuri. She lives across the street from me in Bushwick."

I just smile and nod.

"What up, Zuri!" one of the white boys calls out.

I leave Darius on the sidewalk and make my way into the brownstone, where the smell of alcohol smacks me in the face and the music is really good. The living room has a chandelier, tall bookcases, and strange artwork on the walls. The lights are mostly turned off, and kids are packed tightly into a long hallway that spills into the kitchen at the back of the house. But nobody's dancing. Well, some people are moving their bodies, but it's definitely not what we call dancing around my way.

Carrie is sitting on a leather couch with a red cup in her hand. Our eyes meet. Her mouth drops open. I guess Darius didn't tell her that I was coming to her party. We stare at each other for a minute too long before I blink away and notice the other people around her. Two guys are on the floor in front of her, playing a video game, and she's surrounded by white girls who all have red plastic cups in their hands.

Carrie mouths, "That's her," to one of them. They stare at me. I stare and cock my head to the side. They quickly look away.

There are four other black girls besides me and Carrie. One of them is standing by a marble fireplace. She smiles at me. I smile back. Another one is sitting on a white boy's lap in the corner of the room, and the two others are taking turns swigging from a plastic vodka bottle and giggling.

I stop before I reach the dining room, where another wide chandelier hangs from the ceiling and a long wooden table is pushed aside and covered with snacks, boxes of pizza, and more alcohol.

Someone jumps in front of me—a dark-haired white boy with a huge crooked smile on his face. "Hey, girl! What can I get you?"

"Hey, girl?" I quickly say. "I'm not your girl. My name is Zuri, and I'm good. Thank you."

The boy smiles even bigger, nods, looks me up and down, and says, "Spicy! I like you. You sure you don't wanna get white-boy wasted?"

"Nah. Really. I'm good," I say.

"Careful now," another guy says as he walks up behind the first boy. "That's Darius's girl."

"Darius! This you?" the boy calls out, just as Darius walks

into the house with a line of girls trailing behind him.

Carrie quickly gets up from the couch, goes over to Darius, and hugs him as if he's her man. She talks and laughs too loud and fixes his jacket. And Darius does nothing—nothing to at least show me that he's not cool with it, and that he's here with me.

Someone hands him a red cup, and he takes it. A crowd gathers, and they ask him about Bushwick. Is it safe? Is it loud? Are there gangs? Did he meet any drug dealers? I can tell they're not all serious questions, but just by asking them, they're making fun of my hood.

So I walk over to the group and say, "It's safe, it's loud, there are crews and dope boys. Anything else you wanna know about Bushwick?"

Darius chuckles and shakes his head. "Yeah, Bushwick is cool," he says to his friends. "If I throw a party, will you guys come?"

One of the white boys around him yells out, "Hell, yeah!" Then he starts with "Bushwick! Bushwick! Bushwick!"

I roll my eyes hard at this boy, and I wish Darius would say something to shut him up. He's not focused on me, clearly, even though this was supposed to be a date. I try to make eye contact with the black girl standing by the fireplace. She's dancing by herself with her eyes closed and all.

I go over to her and tap her on the shoulder. "Hi" is all I say.

"Hi," she says, still dancing.

"You know all these people?" I ask.

"Yeah. Pretty much." She sounds like Georgia and Carrie. Her statements sound like questions.

"They all go to Easton?" I ask.

"Easton, Packer, Brooklyn Friends, Poly Prep, Tech, Beacon . . ."

"Oh. Those are private schools?"

"They're just schools," she says, and looks me up and down.

"Bushwick High," I say.

"Cool," she says with a genuine smile.

Her smile lets me know that she's not too stuck-up. I can't blame her for giving me these short answers, because she doesn't know me like that. But we may know somebody in common. "Darius is really popular, huh?"

"Yeah," she says, nodding really hard. "That's an understatement."

"Really? Like, how?"

"I mean, look at him."

And I do. He's not much taller than everyone else, but something about the way he stands and looks around at everybody makes him seem taller. He holds his head up high, nods during a conversation as if that person is saying the most important thing in the world, laughs on cue—throwing his head back and all—and folds his arms and puts his hand back into his pockets at just the right times. He doesn't dance, even as the other kids around him dance. When another song comes on, he just bops his head to the bass. I don't know if he sees me. And at this point, I don't feel like I'm even in the room anymore.

I grab a red plastic cup from a nearby table, pour myself some cranberry juice, and start dancing alone like the girl near the fireplace. I let my body ride the bass, and I mouth the lyrics to myself. I sip and dance, and dance and sip, without a care in the world. But I can't front for too long because Darius walks over. He starts dancing too. He's actually dancing, and I have to stop for a minute to watch him raise his arms and sway to the beat just right. He mouths the lyrics too, and holds his head as if the bass has taken over him. Soon he has a crowd around him again, cheering him on. And I'm ignored, like I'm some side chick he brought with him to show off to his friends.

"Hey, hey, hey!" Darius says, off-key.

"Hey, hey, hey!" everyone sings. But it's all wrong. It's out of tune and off beat.

Nothing about this whole scenario seems legit. Something about the way Darius is moving, the way people are acting around him, and the way he's smiling, lets me know that he's being phony. And that's not the Darius I want to be around—I want the real him, the one I know.

So I put down my cup and tug at his arm. "Sorry to interrupt the Darius Show, but can I talk to you for a second?" I walk out of the house and back down the front steps onto the sidewalk. He follows me with a tight look on his face, but he won't come down the steps all the way. He sits on the stoop instead, still with the red cup in his hand, and with his shifting jaw. "What's this about, Zuri?" he asks.

"No, what was *that* all about, Darius?" I ask.

He puts his hands up and shrugs. "We're at a party. I'm partying. And you?"

"That's what you call *partying*? You're putting on a show in there, Darius!"

He chuckles. "What are you talking about?"

"I'm talking about this!" I try to mock him. I laugh like him and put my hands in my invisible pockets, and cock my head back, and rub my nonexistent hard jawline. I pretend to dance like I have no rhythm at all. "Hey, you guys! You should come see my big house in the ghetto," I say with a fake deep voice.

"Well, you're not a very good actor, 'cause that's not how I look or sound."

"Well, that's how I see you."

"Oh, okay, then. This must be how you want me to party!" He gets up from the stoop, claps his hands in front of my face, snaps his fingers over and over again, rolls his neck and his eyes with his hand on his hip, and says with a fake high voice, "Yeah, bitches and niggas! I'm here to *parrrrtay*!"

"What? Oh, no, you did not just go there!" I shout. "You're gonna stand here and say the n-word in front of these white people's houses, Darius? Typical. I was right about you. You've never heard those words come out my mouth like that. Especially in a place like this." And I purposely snap my fingers, rolling my eyes and neck.

Darius shakes his head, just as Carrie peeks out from the front door. "Hey, Darius. Is everything okay?" she asks, without even looking at me.

"Yeah," Darius says with way more bass in his voice than I've ever heard. And he's still looking dead at me. "I'm good."

I stare at Carrie, but she avoids my eyes. After a long second, she finally goes back inside.

"I wouldn't say those words around my friends," Darius says quietly, almost whispering.

"And I do. But not those kinda friends," I say, but not as quietly.

"What are you saying, Zuri?"

"I'm saying that you were a little extra in there."

"Extra? I'm just being myself!" He's louder now, and his voice cracks.

"Well, that was not the you I've gotten to know these past few days."

He chuckles. "The operative words here are 'past few days.' You don't really know me, Zuri."

"And you don't really know me. 'Cause if you did, you wouldn't bring me someplace like this." And I start to walk away. I'm not sure where I'm going, but there's a busy intersection at the end of the block.

"Zuri, wait," Darius says. "What do you mean 'especially in a place like this'? This is somebody's house, not friggin' . . .

Lincoln Center. I brought you here for a reason."

"And what's that, Darius?" I turn around, cross my arms, and look him in the face, because I know this boy is about to come out the side of his neck with some nonsense. And I am not afraid to tell him about himself.

"To expand your world, Zuri! To party with different kinds of kids. That's what I'm doing. *Partying!*"

"*Partying?* I know how to party, Darius. And I don't need to be around different kinds of kids to party. And you said this was a date, but you left me over here high and dry. That's not what dates do, Darius!"

He steps closer to me, and I don't move back.

"Not everything is about your little corner in the hood. These are kids I go to school with, and I wanted you to meet them. And yes, this was supposed to be a date." He lowers his voice on the last thing he says.

"A date?" I whisper. "Yeah. Maybe you're right. 'Cause dates are for when two people get to know each other better. And I damn sure have gotten to know you better."

He puts his hands up as if he's surrendering. "I'm being myself, Zuri. What do you want? This is me when I'm around people I know, people I'm comfortable with."

"You must not have been comfortable with me, 'cause that's not how you were acting before." I cross my arms and shake my head. "I want to go home."

"What?"

"This isn't for me. I don't feel right in here."

He takes my hand. "Zuri. Come on. Don't be this way."

I pull my hand away again and shake my head. "I was right about you, Darius. We're just too different. This can't work," I whisper.

I walk away. I can feel that Darius doesn't follow me. I make it down to the end of the tree-lined block where the street sign says that it's Fifth Avenue. Everything around is so damn different, clean, and bright, so I close my eyes and try to shut it out. I need to be back in my neighborhood. I need be on my block, in my apartment, and in my bedroom with my sisters.

I know my place. I know where I come from. I know where I belong.

TWENTY-FIVE

PAPI ALWAYS TELLS me to never let the streets know when you're upset. Don't let any strangers see you cry. Hold your head up and look as if you're ready to destroy the world if you have to. Even though part of me wishes I was curled up in my bed and crying right now, I gotta hold it in, because this isn't my hood and I don't really know where I'm going and I can't be looking weak out here.

But tears are welling up in my eyes as I walk down Fifth Avenue toward the Atlantic Center Mall. It's already dark, but the street has a bunch of restaurants where the tables and seats are outside on the sidewalk and I can see right into these people's glasses of wine and plates of fancy pizza.

I replay the whole night over and over in my head, and how I hated seeing Darius act like that. He was the only black guy up in there, and he was acting like he was on stage. This must be how he is in that all-white school of his. This must be how he thinks he needs to be.

I reach the Atlantic Center Mall, and I feel like I can finally breathe. Now these are my people. I can't believe how in just a few blocks, it can feel like two different worlds. I walk over to the G train so I can hop on the L back into my part of Brooklyn, and I scroll through Instagram on my phone while I wait on the platform.

I pause on a photo of Warren and realize that I forgot to unfollow him. It's a close-up of a girl's lips on his neck. I go straight to his page to see a bunch of recent photos from some outdoor party. Of course there's a lot of white people around. And that's when I spot a photo with a black girl sitting on his lap. I look away from my phone, thinking that my eyes must be deceiving me.

"Hold up," I say out loud, and expand one of the photos. "Oh, hell no!"

I have to zoom in to make sure that the little face I've known all my life, the little face I've washed in the morning, rubbed Vaseline on in the winter, and watched cry, smile, and laugh out loud is really in that photo, covered in makeup, and not where it's supposed to be.

"May I speak with you for a minute?" a voice just a few inches from me asks.

I see Darius's sleek sneakers in front of me and look up. He must've followed me all the way over here. A small part of me is happy to see his face.

Still in shock, I hand Darius my phone with the screen opened up to Warren and Layla's picture.

"Wait, is that Layla?" He quickly gives my phone back to me. "That's Carrie's backyard." He runs a hand through his hair in frustration. "What the fuck."

"I need to go get her. Now," I say.

"Okay" is all he says.

Darius hails a cab outside the shopping center. In the cab, I call Layla's phone. No answer. I call Kayla, no answer. I text both of them. *Layla, I'm coming to get you!*

I don't realize that my knee is shaking until Darius puts his hand on it. I quickly push it away.

"I'm sorry," he whispers.

I don't say anything.

We reach Carrie's house, and there's way more people trying to get in now, and the music is louder. I jump out of the cab and push past the people in the doorway.

"Hey!" someone calls out. "She's back!"

"Zuri, wait!" I hear Darius yell behind me. But I ignore him. If Warren is the sleazy bastard that Darius says he is, then

239

I need him away from my little sister.

Darius stops me as I get into the living room. The place is now jam-packed and smoky. And I spot a few more black people, so this must be a legit party now.

"Let's check upstairs," Darius says. He reaches for my hand again, but I don't take it.

"So I don't lose you in the crowd," he says.

"I'm fine, really," I say. "Let's split up."

He nods and disappears upstairs.

I wander through the living room, to the kitchen, and out to the backyard, showing everyone that picture of Layla and Warren on IG, and asking around if they've seen this girl. Some ignore me, the rest shake their heads. Until someone taps me on the shoulder and tells me to check the bathroom downstairs.

I push back through the crowd, my heart pounding in my chest. The basement stairs are hidden behind a group of kids taking shots. When I get down those stairs, I spot Carrie. "Where is she?" I blurt out.

She motions for me to follow her into a giant, fancy bathroom, and I immediately run to my little sister, who's hunched over the toilet.

"Layla! What happened to you?"

"Shots of cognac happened to her," Carrie says.

"What the fuck!" I yell out.

Layla shushes me and laughs.

I check her clothes. She's wearing a fitted tank top I've never seen before and short shorts. She's still dressed, thank goodness.

"She's okay, really," Carrie says.

"She's thirteen!" I yell at her.

"I'm okay!" Layla yells back.

"You won't be if Mama and Papi find out about this."

Layla gets up and sits on the edge of the bathtub. "I didn't do anything I didn't want to, Zuri."

"You wanted Warren to be all over you like that? I saw those pictures, Layla!"

She shrugs. "I like him," she mumbles.

I look over at Carrie. She sighs and says, "Layla, Warren has a bad reputation. So you should be really careful around him."

"*Now* you tell her?" I say.

"Hey! I've been looking out for her this whole time."

Layla points to Carrie and blurts out, "I like you!"

"Did he hurt you?" I ask.

"I'm fine!" Layla slurs her words.

"You're thirteen. You don't know what you're doing. You're not supposed to be drinking and changing your clothes and kissing boys who are four years older than you!"

"That's because Mama and Papi don't let me do anything! You get to have a boyfriend. Janae gets to have a boyfriend. And me and Kayla are supposed to just sit in the house all day? I didn't need you to come save me, Zuri!"

I sigh and shake my head. "Look. Did Warren take any pictures of you?"

"Yeah. And?"

"Naked pictures of you?"

"No! I wouldn't let him do that!"

I exhale.

Carrie crosses her arms and cocks her head to the side. "I know what happened to Georgia. I wouldn't let that happen to your sister."

"Thank you," I manage to say.

I put my arm around my sister and pull her to standing, just as some shouting and yelling make Carrie run out of the bathroom. "Oh god, what now?" she mumbles.

A white boy pokes his head in and shouts, "Fight!"

Layla stumbles up the stairs, and I'm right behind her. People are making their way outside the brownstone and onto the street. I spot two boys on the sidewalk; everyone is trying to move out of their way.

Darius and Warren.

As I get closer to the fight, I see that Darius is lost in a rage. He's got Warren by the collar. Warren pulls away and gets ready to throw a punch, but Darius ducks and hits him with an uppercut. They both step back and dance around each other. Darius gets hit in the face and stomach, but Warren manages to dodge all of Darius's empty punches. No one stops them.

"Hey, hey, hey!" I yell out, and just about jump on Darius's back, trying to pull him away from Warren. I hold him with all my might, and only then does some other black guy pull Warren away.

A few kids help me get Darius back inside the house, because he's still seething. Carrie brings him a glass of water and a pack of frozen peas for his jaw. She goes back and returns with glasses for me and Layla too.

I touch her hand and say, "Seriously. Thank you."

She smiles and nods.

All Is Fair in Love and Warren

I don't need no knights in shining armor
Ain't no horses in the hood
I killed chivalry myself with a pocketknife
A mean mug and a bad mood.

I don't need you to fight my battles
'Cause I've already won this war
Got brothas hollering at me from the corner
Then curse me out when they get ignored.

But if you step to that brotha
Who disrespected me with his eyes
Pull out your fists and throw an uppercut
Like you're some superhero in disguise.

243

I'll look at you twice, maybe three times or four
Secretly cheer you from the sidelines
As you throw another brotha down on the floor.

You've got this whole white audience
Watching this fight like some sport
So to whom do I pledge allegiance
To my heart or to this war?

TWENTY-SIX

MY STOMACH SINKS when I hear sirens coming down the block. It's not the same as hearing sirens in my hood. In this part of Brooklyn, with its giant oak trees and multimillion-dollar brownstones, police and ambulance sirens mean that something really did go down. A police car pulls up to the curb outside Carrie's house.

I just hope no one tells the police that two black boys at this party started all this mess and it ended in a fight.

Carrie is pacing up and down the living room. She's on the phone with her mother, who's on the other side of the world in Paris. Soon two cops are at the door, and I tell Darius to go hide in the bathroom.

"Why?" he asks as he holds the pack of frozen peas to his jaw.

"Because . . ." is all I say.

But Carrie doesn't let them in. She insists that everything's okay and the party's over. The cops mumble something, and in seconds, they're gone.

"Wow. That's it?" I say as Carrie walks back into the living room.

"What do you mean, that's it?" Darius says.

I sigh and shake my head at Darius. "You don't get it," I whisper.

"Yes, I do," he says. "That's it. And that's all that *should* happen."

I shake my head. "Different planet," I say. "What you think *should* happen is what actually happens."

He just narrows his eyes at me. There's a small scratch across his forehead, and his lip is busted. His face is all wound up, and he winces as he gets up from the couch. I stare at him with almost-new eyes, because he's not as cocky when he's in pain.

Layla is sprawled out on another leather couch, and she looks a hot mess too. "I gotta get her home," I say.

"Try to make her eat," Carrie says. "And, wait. Lemme give you something." She rushes back to the kitchen and comes back with a plastic bag and hands it to me. "She's probably gonna throw up again, so you should be prepared."

Darius sits in the front seat to give Layla space to stretch out her legs in the back of the cab. She cracks stupid jokes during the whole ride. And she almost throws up on me and all over the back seat, so Carrie's plastic bag comes in handy.

"She is so wasted. How am I going to get her past my parents?" I ask Darius.

"How 'bout if the cab lets us off around the corner or down the block?" Darius asks while massaging his sore hand. "She can walk it off."

"You kidding me? My whole neighborhood has eyes."

I get a text from Janae, letting me know that everybody's home except for me and Layla. I text her back that Layla's in trouble, so Marisol came up with some lie about Layla being at some friend's party and me promising to pick her up. For whatever reason, my parents always believe Marisol.

"She needs water, food, and sleep," Darius says. "She'll just have to deal with the consequences later."

My stomach twists even tighter at the thought of having to explain all this to my parents. They won't get mad; they'll be disappointed. They'll blame themselves. They'll think back on all the things they've done wrong as young parents. Papi will get even stricter with all of us, and he'll probably cut back on his work hours even more, just so he can keep an eye out on us girls.

"Oh my god," I mumble, holding my head in my hand.

"It'll be that bad, huh?" Darius asks. "Okay. How about we bring her to my house?"

"No way! Your parents *and* my parents will definitely catch us!"

"They're asleep. No one will notice, promise." He shrugs. "Look, Layla can chill there for a while until she can at least stand straight. You can sneak back home with her before dawn."

I shake my head, knowing that at this point, we'll still get in trouble. It's just a matter of how much trouble. I text Janae, letting her know that Layla is okay, and beg her not to say a word to our parents. I call Mama and she doesn't answer, thank goodness.

I lean back against the seat and exhale as the cab drives up to our block.

We reach the side door to the Darcy house. My heart pounds as I look all up and down the block for any of Papi's friends, or Mama's friends too. If Mama and Papi come knocking on the Darcys' door and find Layla drunk, so be it. But if I can save them a heart attack or two, I will.

Darius helps Layla out of the car and walks her to the side door while I cover Layla's mouth, because now she's singing some random song. Soon we're in a lit foyer with hooks along the walls and a metal rack filled with shoes that I notice are Darius's. He fumbles with his keys again, opening a second door that leads down into the basement.

There's a black leather couch in the center with a giant flat-screen TV along the wall. Layla quickly plops her body down, groans, and mumbles something.

"This is my room. Please make yourself at home." Darius

leaves and walks up a flight of stairs at the other end of the basement, and I kneel down in front of Layla to rub her forehead. "You're stupid, you know that?" I say.

She moans. "I'm sorry, Zuri."

"Warren kept giving you drinks, huh?"

"No. I kept asking for them. And I only had two!"

"Stay away from Warren, please."

"Why? He likes me. And I like him."

"I don't care. Stay away from him."

"You can't tell me what to . . . ow!" She rubs her head and squints her eyes.

"See? That's what you get. If Mama and Papi find out about this, it won't matter who likes who. The only boyfriends you'll have are the four walls in our bedroom," I say, while rubbing her back. "And please don't throw up on this couch and give Darius a reason to hate me more."

"I don't hate you, Zuri," Darius says as he walks into the room with a lined trash bin and places it in front of the couch. He hands Layla a glass of water, and I glance up at him. He looks away. I look away.

"You got two hours, Layla," I say as she curls herself up on the couch and closes her eyes. "And then you gotta pull yourself together so we can go home."

She doesn't answer. I shake my head, stand up, and nudge her gently. She moans, so I leave her alone.

It hadn't crossed my mind that I'd have to wait for Layla

while she sobers up. I didn't ever think I'd be in the Darcy house again. Especially after our fight.

I look around his room and realize that it's not at all what I expected. It's way more . . . him. A video-game console and controllers sit on a gray rug in front of the couch. Canvases—some blank, some painted on, some drawn on—are all over the basement. Some are propped against the walls, some are hanging, and some are stacked up on a wide wooden table in the far corner of the basement. There are glass jars of paintbrushes in all sizes along the edge of the table. In another corner are a bass guitar and a keyboard.

Darius walks through a door at the other end of the basement, and I can spot a giant bed in that room. He comes out with a plaid blanket that he gently throws over Layla.

"Thank you," I say. I cross my arms because I don't know what else to do with myself in this place. Then I ask, "You paint? Why didn't you tell me?"

"I took painting classes at school and I liked it. It calms me a little. But playing music energizes me. Balance." Then he points to a closed door on the opposite side of the basement. "That's Ainsley's room over there."

"So it's like you two have a whole basement apartment to yourselves?" I say.

"Yeah, we designed it that way. I mean, that's why my parents wanted a big house. We lived in a small two-bedroom apartment in Manhattan, so . . ."

"So . . . I don't know what you're talking about, because me and my sisters share one room."

"Zuri." He sighs, still massaging his hand. "I can't change anything about my life. . . ."

"Sorry," I say, knowing exactly what he means by that. I sigh, look down, then look up at him. "You should do something about that. Do you have ice?"

He walks to a dark corner and turns on a light. He opens a small fridge and pulls out an ice tray. He holds an ice cube in his hand.

I laugh and shake my head. "Lemme help you with that. You got some sort of towel?"

He motions for me to follow him into his bedroom. I hesitate a little bit, but my legs have already agreed, because I walk in to see how beautiful his room is. High windows line the walls. There are hanging plants everywhere, and a giant fish tank sits along the wall. His bed is pushed up against the far wall, and it's actually neat, with the covers pulled up and everything. The sound of running water from the fish tank makes the whole room feel peaceful. Shelves are mounted on every available surface, with books stacked up to the ceiling.

"So you're an artist, a musician, a green thumb, a fish lover, and a reader?" I ask. "That's sure a lot of stuff for someone who once told me they like empty spaces."

"What can I say? It's my little oasis," he says, plopping down on his bed.

"Your oasis in the hood, huh? It's just so different from the rest of the house."

"Well, I'm different from the rest of the house," he says. He motions for me to come sit next to him, but I don't.

I spot a giant floor pillow in the corner, pick it up, and place it a little close to his bed, but not too close. "Different? Coulda fooled me."

"I did fool you, didn't I?" he says, pulling open a dresser, grabbing a T-shirt, and wrapping it around the ice. He holds it to his hand. "Sit on the bed. I don't want my guest sitting on the floor."

So we switch spots, and his bed is the softest thing I've ever sat on in my life. But I don't let myself get too comfortable. I spot a picture of him as a little boy on his dresser—scrawny, wearing glasses, and with a thick book in his hand.

I sigh and roll my eyes. "I guess you did fool me. But you really didn't have to get into a fight with Warren."

"Yes I did. I've been waiting for another reason to bust him in his face."

"Oh, so it wasn't about looking out for my sister?"

"It was. I wouldn't want what happened to Georgia to happen to Layla," he says.

"Layla?" I ask. "What about me? He could've pulled that shit with me. I wouldn't let him, but still."

He bites his busted bottom lip and hangs his head down. "I didn't think of that. You were so . . ." He inhales.

"So what? So tough? So bitchy?" I smile. "And too what? Too stuck-up? Too conceited?"

"All of the above." He cocks his head back a little bit when he says this. But his eyes are soft, as if he's owning up to everything that he is.

Or everything I thought he was.

"What are you saying? I was right about you? I thought you fooled me," I say, looking down at my own hands and not at his soft eyes.

"I thought I was trying to fool you." He inhales and leans in a little bit. "Zuri, you don't think I know that this is the hood and guys around here would be messing with me and my brother? You don't think I knew that I'd have a reputation as soon as I stepped out of that car? And I knew it wouldn't be street rep, either. I saw it all over your face, Zuri. You couldn't stand me. And according to you, Warren was your boy in the hood. Who was I to mess that up for you?"

I bite the inside of my cheek, still not looking at Darius. There's some old blue nail polish left on my thumbnail, and I pick at that.

"Hey?" Darius says, lowering his head to make eye contact with me.

My body starts to feel weird. And I know this feeling. My insides are melting into sweet, gooey, sticky honey. So I quickly stand up from his bed. "I should check on Layla."

"Give her a few minutes," he says, while trying to get up

too. He scrunches his face and holds the side of his belly.

I reach for his hand and help him up. When he does, we're standing face-to-face. Sort of, because he's taller than me. His lips are where my forehead is, so he quickly kisses it, as if that's what I was asking him to do.

I step back.

"I'm sorry," he says. "I didn't mean to . . ."

"It's okay," I say. "I can't be in here."

He grabs my hand. "I get it. It's cool. Let me show you something."

I give him a surprised look as he pulls me out of his bedroom, past a sleeping Layla, and up the stairs leading out of the basement. He turns around and places his finger over his lips, as if I would dare say anything now.

The house is dark, but there are tiny dim lights all over that are enough for us to tiptoe our way up two flights of stairs. My heart is racing and my hand starts to sweat in his hand. My mind is racing with all kinds of thoughts about how this is not a good idea. But my insides seem to have taken over my brain, and in seconds, we're walking up a short flight of concrete steps to the roof of his house.

There's no ladder, no rusty metal door, no tar or blue tarp here. It's as if this is a whole backyard, complete with a wide canopy, outdoor furniture, plants, and string of gold and silver Christmas lights that Darius turns on from some hidden spot. It all takes my breath away.

"Wow," I whisper. "I didn't know all this was up here."

"You thought you knew everything, huh?" Darius says. He sits down on a wicker couch in the middle of the roof. There's also a rug and wicker coffee table. It's a straight-up whole other apartment on his roof!

"Yeah," I say, nodding. "I did."

He laughs and motions with his head for me to join him. I don't think twice about it, because the sky here seems wider. And maybe there are more stars from this view. And maybe the moon shines brighter. Maybe everything is better from the roof of the Darcy house.

He eases closer to me when I sit down. We're quiet for a long moment, and I realize I can see the top of my building from here. "Did you ever see . . . ," I start to ask.

"Yep," he says. "You and Janae would just sit there and laugh and probably talk about me and Ainsley. . . ."

"No, we weren't talking about you," I lie.

"You were trying to throw tiny meatballs at this house."

"You saw that?" I laugh and cover my mouth.

"I saw you," he says quietly.

I just stare at him when he says this, and he stares back. Neither of us looks away.

"ZZ. Girl in the hood," he says.

"Darius Dorky," I say.

He laughs. "*Dorky?* I'm dorky?"

"Yes, you are." I laugh.

I'm fidgeting with my hands again, and he takes one of them.

"Zuri, I'm not going to try to be hard or pretend I'm from the hood. My parents protected us from all that. They raised us how they were raised. I mean, you met my grandmother. She has big dreams for me and Ainsley. I can't help that, and I can't change that." He slips his fingers in between mine, and I let him.

It's as if I've been holding a weapon all this time, ready to defend myself if he said anything wrong, and he just pulled it out of my hand, disarming me.

"I don't know about that life, Darius. That run-down building over there has been my home since forever. My parents work hard too, and they do not treat people like shit. Nobody on my block does, and if they do, there's somebody to call them out on it. We're like family. You treated me and my sisters like shit, and I needed to call you out on it. And I can't help that or change that."

"But I wasn't . . ." He pulls my hand toward him a little bit.

"Darius."

"You judged me too. You treated me and my brother like shit too." Now he places his other hand over mine.

"No, I wasn't . . ."

"Zuri."

"Okay. Fine," I say.

"Can we start over?" he asks. Then he brings my hand to his lips and kisses it.

My insides turn warm, and there's nothing left to do but close my eyes and let my whole self melt in his hands, against his lips. "No, we cannot," I whisper. "We're not gonna just throw away the past as if it meant nothing. See? That's what happens to whole neighborhoods. We built something, it was messy, but we're not gonna throw it away."

"Touché. I like that analogy." He squeezes my hand a little.

"I wasn't trying to impress you," I say.

"Well, I've been impressed. From day one." He turns his whole body to me now, still with my hand in his.

I slowly pull my hand away from his.

"But I live in your neighborhood. I haven't thrown anything or anyone away."

I close my eyes for a moment and inhale. "Do you see that rent is going up all over the place and people are not getting paid more? Schools are shitty because teachers think we're a lost cause. I'm trying to get into college, but I need financial aid and scholarships 'cause I have three more sisters who want to go to college too, and my parents have always been broke. That's why I had a wall up with you. You were moving into my hood from what seemed like a whole different world."

We're both quiet for a long minute before he says, "I under-stand. But it's not like I have it easy, either."

"Darius, if my family had your kind of money and this kind of house, my whole life would've been different."

After what feels like forever, he says, "I never told you this, but we left our old apartment on the Upper East Side because the neighbors had concerns about me and Ainsley. We had lived there since we were toddlers. Everybody thought we were cute when we were in the third grade. But once we got taller and got some bass in our voices, they decided that they didn't recognize us anymore. So we decided to move. But I dunno, sometimes I still feel like I don't belong in Bushwick, either. I don't fit in anywhere."

"But I don't want you to, Darius. I just want you to be you and me to be me." I wrap my fingers through his.

He smiles, just a little bit. "If you say so," he says.

"What do we do now, then?" I ask.

"I have an idea," he says. He's closer to me now. Our legs are touching.

And finally he leans in and kisses me. He eases his fingers across my cheek, up around my neck, toward the back of my head, and through the tight coils of my hair. He cradles my head in his hand as he kisses me deep, deep. I am honey again.

It all feels like the end of a game that we didn't even know we were playing. And we've both had the ball stolen and thrown back, played defense and offense. And from the way he kisses me—easing his bruised hand around my body and pulling me in close, almost swallowing me with his whole self—I know that I've won this game. And he's won too.

I almost fall asleep in Darius's arms, on this roof, across the street from my own building. The nearby sirens will put me into an even a deeper sleep if I let them, but it's the flashing lights behind my closed eyelids that make me pull away from Darius's warmth and slow-beating heart.

He's awake too, squinting. "I think there's an ambulance in front of your building," he says.

"Oh, shit!" I say, and I'm on my feet and ready to rush down from the roof. But he quickly gets in front of me to open the door.

"Darius? Is that you?" his mother calls out from a nearby room when we reach the second floor.

"Yeah, Mom," he says. "Was just hanging out on the roof for a bit. Going to bed."

His mother says good night, and we tiptoe back down to the basement, where Layla is just starting to toss about.

"Layla, we gotta go," I say, nudging her.

She gets up groggy and confused, but Darius helps us up the stairs and out the door. We have to decide in a split second whether or not he'll walk me across the street.

"I'm coming with you," he says.

I nod and swallow hard.

Just as we come around his house, I spot Mama and Papi in our open doorway as two EMT workers bring a stretcher down the front stoop. There's a body on that stretcher. I look at Mama and Papi, and it takes me a second to make sure that they're both standing there and not on that stretcher.

My heart sinks, and I'm frozen where I stand, with Layla leaning her head on my shoulder.

"What's going on?" she asks, slowly pulling away from me. Then it hits her. "Oh my god, no!"

She rushes across the street, and it takes me a while to follow her, because my legs feel like tree trunks. I can't move them.

Marisol, Kayla, and Janae come out of the building. Janae is the first to spot me across the street, and she motions for me to hurry up.

I once asked Madrina how she knows so much about the strangers who come down to the basement for her love consultations. She told me that thoughts and feelings are vibrations. They move the air like a light breeze, and if I pay close enough attention, I can feel those thoughts in my own body. So even with the white sheet covering her whole body and her face, I already know. And I'm the first to fall to my knees and start crying.

Never in my life have I wanted to disappear into thin air as I do now. But not because Papi's eyes have disappointment written all over them. Not because Mama's eyes are red and teary and she doesn't even look at me or Darius. Not because my sisters try to console me and even Janae comes down to the ground with me and hugs me tight.

I was on the roof with Darius when Madrina's spirit left the world. Our bodies were glued together and I was happy for a little while, but I didn't know that this deep sadness was waiting for me like an open door.

And then I think that it was maybe Madrina, priestess of the love goddess Ochún, who made it so. She gave me that little bit of happiness.

TWENTY-SEVEN

Elegy for Paola Esperanza Negrón
or
¡Ay Madrina! ¡Mi madrina!

¡Ay Madrina! ¡Mi madrina!
The very last drumbeat has left its mark.
Its pulsing rhythm leaves no sound,
like blown-out candles in the dark.
The singing voices muted,
the quiet prayers unheard,
the orishas have retreated,
your shining light now blurred.
    ¡Pero mi corazón! ¡Mi corazón!

The only music left
against the melody of my own song,
to my sweet Ochún, of love, bereft.

¡Ay Madrina! ¡Mi madrina!
Who will clear these lovers' paths
to walk these noisy streets
where toppled buildings unearth our wrath?
Newcomers fill these spaces
with shiny jewels and polished stone.
We blacks and browns have surrendered,
while our memory stands alone.
¡Ahora, Madrina! ¡Querida abuela!
This is the greatest theft.
Los antepasados have stolen you
from my sweet Ochún, of love, bereft.

I get applause after reading my poem, the loudest from Colin, who gives a whistle. Every word rolled out of my mouth heavy and hard like the round red-and-white mint candies Madrina used to give me. I take my seat in the front-row pew.

There's standing room only at St. Martin of Tours Roman Catholic church on Hancock Street, and it's a sea of all shades of brown people wearing either black or white. The ones who wear black are just following the Catholic tradition. The ones who wear white are following the Santería tradition. But everyone's here to celebrate Madrina in their own special way.

I too am dressed in all white from head to toe, and Madrina would've liked that. My hair is wrapped beneath one of her head scarves. And even though I'm not supposed to wear them because a santera or santero hasn't blessed them and I haven't made ocha, her colorful elekes hang long around my neck. Every single one of them. And I'll cut my eyes at any santero who questions me.

I know almost everybody who's come to her funeral, including Darius, who walked in while I was reciting my poem. I had to pause for a long second, almost forgetting the words that were right there on the page.

Afterward, Mama opens up our apartment and the whole building for the repast. She's been cooking for three days, and my sisters and I have been helping her. And when the church doors open so everyone can make their way to our building, I hear the congas. My heart leaps. Bobbito, Manny, and Wayne have gathered about a dozen drummers to play outside the church.

I take Darius's hand so everyone around can see that we're together, and we walk toward the drums. The santeras do a little two-step as they lead the procession from the church to our building. They smile at me and Darius as we walk hand in hand.

"Paola has blessed you before she left this side, I see," one of them says to me. I only smile and glance at Darius.

Janae is waiting for me at the corner on Knickerbocker. She

looks at both of our faces, and I can't tell if she's happy for us or not. But still, she smiles big and wide when I get closer to her. I let go of Darius's hand so my sister and I can hug.

Practically the whole neighborhood has come out to celebrate Madrina's life. And this is almost like a parade for her.

"How you holding up, sis?" Charlise asks when she joins us. "I know Colin is taking it rough. Madrina was like his real mom. I can't believe she left him the building! And for her to go—" She snaps her fingers. "Just like that."

I shrug and twist my mouth and look around for Colin. I spot him and Papi having a conversation. Papi's body language is telling a story. He's talking with his hands, something he only does when he's really pissed, and he rarely gets really pissed.

Colin hangs his head low, a stance I've never seen him take before. Then Papi reaches out and touches his shoulder in a father-son way. Without thinking twice about it, I start to make my way over there, leaving Darius with Charlise. But by the time I reach them, the conversation is already over.

"Hey" is all I say to Colin.

He's got a look on his face I've never seen before. His brows are furrowed and his arms are crossed. "Hey, Zuri," he almost whispers. Then he flashes me a half smile and walks away.

"Papi, what happened between you and Colin?" I ask.

He's running his hands through his thick, curly hair and he sighs deeply. "It's okay, Zuri. Go be with your friends."

He takes a look around at all the people gathered on the sidewalk in front of our building and the people walking down from Bushwick Avenue and Jefferson. He rubs his graying beard and sighs again.

"Papi, I know when you're not okay," I say.

"Ah, my Zuri Luz, always watching out for your papi, huh?" he says, giving my shoulder a squeeze.

"What are you talking about? What just happened?"

"Let's go for a walk," he says, motioning for me to follow him. Suddenly I'm nervous. Papi is not the kind of man to just go for a stroll. We walk down Jefferson as he waves and says hi to neighbors and friends. "She's singing and dancing in heaven, now," he says when they give him their condolences for Madrina. We weren't her family, but besides Colin, we were the closest thing she had.

When we're past Broadway, Papi sighs for the umpteenth time and says, "Colin's selling the building. A developer offered him a lot of money."

I quickly look up. "What?" I don't understand what he's saying.

"We have to move, Zuri."

"Move? We can't just leave!" My stomach twists as the words come tumbling out of my mouth. Warm tears sting my eyes. I've lost my madrina and now I'm going to lose my home?

"Mija, don't get emotional on me, Zuri. I agreed to the buy-out. We need it."

I gasp and stop walking. Out of all the things Papi could have said, I never imagined those words. A developer? A buyout? Of course, after Madrina died, I wondered who would take care of the building. But I thought Colin would just be our landlord. Not that he'd sell to an outsider.

"Buyout? You sold us out, Papi?"

"We need that money, sweetheart. For our future. I got five of you to take care of. A building is just a building, in the end."

"But how could you? Just like that?" I mumble, tears now streaming freely down my cheeks. Papi pulls me close into a hug, but I am stiff in my father's arms, and angry.

"Well, I had to curse him one or two times, 'cause you know how your papi is. We Benitezes don't take no crap. He gave me a good price. And that was that." He looks down at me and holds me tighter. I start to relax and use his good white shirt to wipe away my tears.

"But Papi, where are we gonna go?"

He lets go of me and shakes his head. "I don't know yet, but we'll find somewhere. This is what happens in life—you take the good with the bad. This money is good. Us leaving is bad. But we're taking it because it's a blessing. You know, like that boy across the street."

I inhale deep, sniffling, and roll my eyes. "You don't know anything about the boy across the street, Papi. Now don't change the subject."

"No secrets in our house, Zuri. You like him, fine. As long

as he likes you too, and most important, he respects you."

"But he gets to stay, Papi," I say quietly, and I realize that Darius will no longer be the boy across the street. He'll still be in Bushwick, and I'll be . . . somewhere else because the rent is too high in my own hood.

"So. And you get to leave. Him and his family are living somewhere new. They get to have new experiences. And you and your sisters, you've been in Bushwick all your lives. I saw that look in Janae's eyes when she came back from college. Her eyes have seen so much more than me and your mother ever have. And you, sweetheart. You were a lightbulb when you came back from D.C. That is what I want for all of you. And myself too. To think, I spent half my life in that tiny apartment. And now, money has fallen from the sky."

I don't like what Papi is saying one bit. He makes sense, but I still don't like it. "What's Colin gonna do with the money anyway? He's only nineteen," I say. A lump is forming in my throat, but I keep swallowing to keep my tears down.

"According to him, Madrina has been getting offers for years. Someone came to him with a deal he couldn't refuse. All cash. Look, Zuri, keep your head up, my daughter. I used to be like you, you know—getting pissed at the world when this or that didn't go my way. But you know what opened up my eyes and my heart? Your mother and five beautiful daughters. The world could fall apart around me, but we are still a family. It doesn't matter where we go. Bushwick will come with us. Don't let your pride get in the way of your heart, mija." He turns to look at me.

With every word he says, the tears start to well up in my eyes again. I keep blinking them back, but my face is wet.

"Hey, mija," Papi says, holding me by the shoulders so that he can look me straight in the eye. "I knew it would be you to take it the hardest. It's a lot, Zuri. First Madrina. And now this. But you gotta grow up. It's a big world out there."

I can't help but laugh a little, even as tears roll down my cheeks. "That was corny, Papi." And then I let it all out. I hang my head low, and the tears fall like rain. I cross my arms.

"No, no, no," he says. "Not out here, and not like this."

We've walked about ten blocks, and I realize where Papi's going. He's headed for the library on Dekalb and Bushwick— our favorite spot. This is where he'd take me when I was little. I'd disappear into the kids' section, and he'd disappear between any and every aisle of thick books. But it's Sunday, and we can tell from the tall and wide windows that the lights are off and it's closed.

The gate leading up to the front steps is wide open, though, so we walk in and sit there.

"You don't wanna leave that boy?" Papi asks. "Darius?"

"Papi!" I say. "I don't wanna leave our hood, our building, our home!"

"And that boy," he says.

Papi knows me through and through. So I hide my face in my hands, not wanting to believe that he's right. "It's more than the boy," I mumble. I look up at him. "Papi, if we could just live on only one floor of his house."

"It's not our house and it's not our life. And who knows? Maybe being here was a tough decision for them too. I mean, it's not like they fit in, you know? And maybe with that buy-out money and all, we'll be the new rich kids on the block. Entiendes?"

I laugh a little again. And Papi places his arm around my shoulders and I lean in to him. He kisses my forehead, and his beard grazes my skin. I have always thought of Bushwick as home, but in that moment, I realize that home is where the people I love are, wherever that is.

TWENTY-EIGHT

AS MY SISTERS begin packing, I spend as much time at the library on Bushwick Avenue as I possibly can. I sit in corners, at tables, on dirty couches, and on the front steps, getting lost in the pages of books. But most important, I work on my essay for Howard University.

College is the one true thing I can hold on to. It's going to happen no matter what. But I can either stay here in Brooklyn and go to a community college, or one of the City University schools, or go away. And the only option I've given myself for going away is Howard. I have to make this happen for myself. If I get in, then I'll know that people like me have a say in how our lives turn out. Even if we're thrown away by people with more money, we can always climb our way out of the messiness and the brokenness of our lives.

Because the thing about sharp corners is, the right turns can bring you back home.

I print out my five-hundred-word essay just as the security guard announces that it's five minutes till closing. I don't write a poem after all, but poetry has helped me get my feelings out. My broken words helped me make sense of everything, so that when I pieced them back together in an essay, my truth was clearer.

I place everything in a folder on my thumb drive with all my other application materials for early acceptance. But before I close it, I start a new document and get some last words out.

Pride
by Zuri Benitez

We were not supposed to be proud. We were not supposed to love these things so hard: the chipping paint, the missing floorboards, the gas stove we have to light with matches, the cracks in the windows, the moldy bathroom tiles, the mice and the roaches.

But I've never known anything else. These broken things all spell home to me.

They are like the many worn sheets and blankets Mama and Papi brought with them from their childhood. They are older than us, and there are stories lodged in their cracks and crevices, their stains and their tears. And if I listen closely enough, I can hear the whispers of the ones who came before us. They've left these holes for us to fill.

Ambulance sirens at night put me to sleep. Cars honking and neighbors cursing at each other let me know that love lives here. We care enough to be angry and impatient. Sometimes I wonder . . . if my neighborhood ever floods or breaks in half, and someone throws me, only me, a lifeboat or a lifeline, will I take it and leave everyone and everything behind?

This college is a lifeboat and a lifeline.

But my neighborhood is not flooding or splitting in half. It's being cleaned up and wiped out. It's being polished and erased. So where do I reach back and pull out memories as if they've been safely tucked away into a trunk or an attic like the people on TV who have enough time and too much space? Where do I call home? Where can I place a layer of brick to use as my platform, and hold my head up high to raise my voice and my fist?

Sometimes love is not enough to keep a community together. There needs to be something more tangible, like fair housing, opportunities, and access to resources. Lifeboats and lifelines are not supposed to just be a way for us to get out. They should be ways to let us stay in and survive. And thrive.

I pause in my typing and look up. All around me, a slight breeze brushes past the back of my neck, and my whole body tingles. It's not like Darius's touch at all. It's more like a presence of something or someone on another side of this reality. And that's when I know for sure that all of Madrina's stories about los antepasados are as real as breath. She is still as real as breath. She is love. She is with me. Me, daughter of Ochún.

TWENTY-NINE

WE DON'T KNOW how to move. We don't know how to pack up our lives into small, medium, and large cardboard boxes.

Mama wants to keep every single thing: baby clothes, our drawings from kindergarten, our cheap Barbie doll knockoffs.

Papi wants to throw out everything. And he does it. But behind Mama's back, so that each time she thinks a box is full and ready to be taped closed, she goes off somewhere and comes back only to find it half empty again. And the last few days have shown me what our family is really made of: we are our memories, our love, and our things.

It's the last day before Janae goes back up to Syracuse. She's taking a box of her favorite things with her, afraid that Papi will throw them out. Me, Nae-nae, Marisol, and the twins are squeezed together on the front stoop. We used to all fit on one step, with our thin thighs and shoulders touching. Then, on two steps.

Now Layla sits on the step below, with her head resting on my right knee as I cornrow her hair. She digs into a small bag of sunflower seeds and spits out the shells on the ground next to the stoop. One lands on Marisol's arm, and she smacks Layla's knee. That would usually turn into an argument, but today, we all know that we don't want to spend this last moment arguing.

It's unusually quiet for a Saturday afternoon, but part of me wonders if the whole block is a little sad that we're leaving. Charlise has already left for Duke, so she's not here to crack jokes and cheer us up a bit. People have come in and out of our building, saying their goodbyes to Mama and Papi, and paying their final respects to Madrina's basement. And maybe this quiet, sunny, warm Saturday afternoon is a long, heavy sigh. And that's exactly what I do as I finish Layla's final braid. In that same moment, the front door to the Darcys' house opens up, and I pretend not to notice, even as all my sisters turn to watch my reaction.

But it's Ainsley who walks out of the building, not Darius.

Ainsley comes over to us the same way Darius usually does, with his hands in his pockets and his shoulders slightly hunched over. But he doesn't share the same hard jawline as Darius. His smile is crooked, his eyes are bright, and his fresh haircut makes him look kind of nerdy. A cute kind of nerdy. In that moment, I realize that Ainsley just might be perfect for my sister Janae.

We all pretend to not be paying him any mind: I brush back Layla's edges, Kayla investigates a sunflower seed, Marisol reads her Suze Orman book, and Janae pretends to be on the phone. But she's not a good actress, because she's trying too hard to keep it cool.

"Hey," Ainsley says to Janae, or all of us. He faces Janae, but he doesn't know which one of us to look at.

"Hey," Janae says back.

"Let's go up to the roof," I say. "It's too hot down here."

"Nuh-uh! It's hotter on the roof 'cause we're closer to the sun!" Layla says without budging.

And I pinch her arm. "Let's go," I say through clenched teeth.

Marisol shakes her head and rolls her eyes at Janae, but she's the first one up the stairs with me and the twins behind her.

"Why we gotta be the ones to leave?" Kayla nags. "We should have that Darcy boy let us stay in his house with that air conditioner if he wants to talk to Janae."

"That's a good idea," Marisol adds as she opens the door leading up the roof. "It'll be like charging money. One hour with Janae costs one hour of going through that big ol' fridge of theirs."

Papi opens the door to the apartment to check in on us.

He has on a mask and gloves while he and Mama clear out the dust from behind the furniture. They wanted us out of the way because we talk and argue too much. He wanted Mama out of the way too, but she got hip to his game of throwing things out behind her back.

"Please, nobody fall, okay?" he says through the mask.

"Madrina's watching over us," I say to him with a smile.

His eyes smile and he shakes his head. Something is a little different about my father now. He's a little happier, a little lighter. This move will be good for him.

On the roof, my sisters ease toward the edge, trying to eavesdrop on Janae and Ainsley's conversation. But I keep looking at the house across the street, wondering if Darius is looking over at us too.

"He's leaving," Layla says. Then she calls out, "Bye, Ainsley!"

I see him wave back from across the street, and I glance at the Darcys' roof again, wondering if Darius was watching it all go down too.

In no time, Janae joins us with a big smile on her face.

"He offered to drive me up to school," she says with a soft, sweet voice.

"What?" I ask, walking over to her.

"His school, Cornell, is about an hour away from Syracuse. So we can go up together. I'll have to squeeze my stuff into his back seat, but . . ." She's grinning hard, clasping her hands, and almost standing on her tippy-toes as if she's a rocket ship about to be launched to the moon. She's about to straight-up burst with happiness.

So I hug her. "Take it slow, okay?" I whisper.

"Z, I have a really good feeling about this," she says, inhaling deep.

"Janae and Ainsley, sitting in a tree!" Kayla starts singing as she pulls out the blue tarp for all of us to sit on.

"K-I-S-S-I-N-G!" Layla adds. "First comes love, then comes marriage . . ."

Janae sits down on the tarp first, rests her chin in her hand, and with a big smile says, "Go on."

"No, stop!" I say. "Don't go on. No love, no marriage, and no baby, Janae! Okay, maybe a little bit of love. But no marriage and no baby."

"It's just a song!" she says, laughing.

I roll my eyes at her as we all squeeze onto the tarp one last time. I put my arm around Janae, and Marisol on the other side of me. We all squeeze in tight, resting our heads on each other's shoulders as the late summer sun sets over Bushwick. The orange sky seems to stretch farther than it ever has. We stay quiet, even the chatty twins, saying our goodbyes like silent prayers.

Each of my sisters leaves one by one, leaving me and Janae to ourselves for the rest of the night. A full moon is out tonight, and this moment feels just as full—almost pregnant. Like our new life is about to be born as we move to Canarsie.

Ainsley is the first thing Janae brings up when we're finally alone.

"Fine, okay, I do think you two make a cute couple," I say, sighing.

"You and Darius look good together too," she says, leaning her head on my shoulder.

"I don't care if we look good together. I care if he's a good person or not."

"Well, is he?"

I look across the street. I close my eyes for a minute to see if I can *feel* Darius watching us from his roof. Madrina always said that love connects two people in ways that we can't even see, but we feel it. I shake that thought from my head and open my eyes, because this isn't love. Not yet, anyway. So I say to Janae, "I don't know. We'll see."

"Well, how long are you giving him? A few days, months, years? A lifetime?"

"How long did you give Ainsley?"

"Long enough for him to come to his senses."

"What if he never did? What if he never said a word to you before you left for Syracuse?"

She inhales deep and waits a long minute before she answers my question. "He would've. If not today, then I would've seen him again. Even if it took a few more months. Or years. I just . . . knew."

Madrina would know.

It's the middle of the night and our bedroom is almost emptied out, with only a few open boxes left. Our mattresses had to be wrapped in plastic and stacked in the living room for the movers in the morning. So we lie on blankets. But I can't sleep.

I sneak down to Madrina's apartment, where the door is unlocked and it's completely empty, but her scent still lingers in the air—cigar and sage smoke, Florida water, incense, and cheap perfume. These smells are even stronger as I make my way down to the basement.

This is no longer Madrina's temple for Ochún. It's as if everything has been poured out into a flowing river.

But Madrina's chair is still there. Stripped of its white fabric and yellow cushion, it's more like a skeleton of itself. I sit in it and fold my hands over my belly, just like Madrina used to. I lean my head back and close my eyes to hear her voice one last time.

Ah, mija! There you go! Rivers flow. A body of water that remains stagnant is just a cesspool, mi amor! It's time to move, flow, grow. That is the nature of rivers. That is the nature of love!

THIRTY

EVERYONE IS DOWNSTAIRS waiting for the moving truck to pull off, and I'm the last to take a tour of the place before I say good-bye forever. I finger a layer of dust on my bedroom windowsill. Our apartment looks way bigger without all the furniture and stuff. And much more broken too. There're cracks in the walls, mold, chipping paint—this crowded apartment probably wasn't good for our health.

The kitchen looks even smaller, though. I can't believe that Mama has cooked all those meals, enough to feed a whole block, in that tiny kitchen. The stove and countertops have been scrubbed clean, and I wonder if it will all be torn away to make room for a bigger kitchen like the one at Darius's house.

I take another look at the whole apartment, inhale deeply,

step outside, and close the door.

I did not want to cry, but the tears burst out of me like a newly opened fire hydrant in the summer. I hug myself and press my head against the closed door. All of me, everything I've ever known and loved, was once behind that door. I feel as if I've stepped outside my own body, and I'm leaving it behind.

"Zuri?" Someone says my name quietly.

I sniff and try to hold back my tears, but I can't. I don't turn around to see who it is, but I know the voice. I don't dare move.

He touches my shoulder. Still I don't move.

"Hey." He gently turns me around.

I cross my arms and don't look up at him.

He pulls me in, hugs me, and kisses my forehead. So I just let it all out again, in his chest, in his arms.

I pull away from him a little and look into his eyes. He wipes the tears from my cheeks with his thumbs and kisses me on the lips.

The very last thing I do in this building is kiss a boy—the boy who moved in across the street and changed everything. Maybe this is what Madrina wanted all along: for me to find love and take it with me when I leave this place.

So we walk down the steps and out of the building hand in hand. Half our block is out on the sidewalk, saying goodbye to my sisters, Mama, and Papi. They all turn to see me and Darius holding hands again. Of course they all have to comment all at once. Some whistle, others cheer, and the rest of them laugh as if we're five-year-olds and this little thing is cute but won't last.

I catch Papi's eyes smiling. He quietly nods and turns away.

Manny from down the block has offered his minivan to drive Mama and my sisters out to our new place. I got dibs on riding with Papi in the moving truck.

Before I hop onto the middle seat between the mover and Papi, Darius pulls me aside again. "I can come pick you up. Take a long drive through Brooklyn. From Canarsie all the way to Brooklyn Heights."

"Nah," I say, shaking my head. "I am not your Brooklyn tour guide, Darius Darcy! You want to come pick me up, take the train."

"How 'bout a cab?"

"No, Darius! The subway. Last stop on the L. You're in Brooklyn now."

"Last stop on the L," he repeats, smiling, and takes the tips of my fingers until I climb into the truck.

Papi takes his hand and gives him a hard dap. "You take care, okay, buddy?"

Then Papi pulls Darius in and gives him one of those homie hugs. This is the thing that melts my heart the most. It's as if my whole neighborhood has said yes to the boy who moved in across the street, to me and him.

Papi, I met this boy.

Even though he's not old enough yet, I know you will
tell him to get a case of Presidente beer from Hernando's
to share on the stoop one last time with this boy
who likes your daughter because you will hope that he
has a heart big enough to love me much more than you
because this is what you want for all of us, Papi.
You want your daughters' boyfriends to have wisdom
as layered as pages in a book, memories as old
as slave ships at the shores of Hispaniola,
and love as endless as bottles of Presidente beer
shared on the stoops all over Bushwick
late into the night, Papi.

I met this boy.

Canarsie really is the very edge of the world, or at least
Brooklyn. It feels that way since it takes so long for me to get to
and from my old neighborhood. My sisters and I have to leave
the house by six thirty in the morning just to get to school on
time. Canarsie is the first and last stop on the L train, just like
Darius said.

My new hood is nothing like my old hood. If there are
newcomers here, they're black or Latinx like our family. No

one is coming here to throw anything away. There's room to spread my arms and not hit anybody in the head. I can go a whole day sitting in front of the house and only see about five people. But no one sits on stoops here. No one pulls out a barbecue grill on the sidewalk, or a small table for a game of dominoes. The bodega is more than five blocks away, and we have to drive to the closest supermarket or Laundromat. But Mama and Papi still don't know how to drive and don't have a car. So most of our days are spent commuting to and from everywhere and stuck inside the small two-story house, minding our own business. Marisol and the twins spend more time at school with extracurricular activities, and Mama cooks way too much food, since our kitchen is much bigger now. Howard University has my new address, and they've been filling our mailbox with catalogs and postcards. I take that as a good sign.

We have more space and less time. And the love we had for our whole neighborhood now only fits into this wood-frame house in the middle of a quiet block. We don't know the people who live across the street or on either side of us.

After my first day of senior year, I take a trip to my old block. Darius has been wanting to come see me, but we still had boxes and I was still trying to make sense of it all. I wanted more than anything to step back onto Jefferson and Bushwick Avenues, but only when I knew I was ready.

Darius meets me at the Halsey Street and Wyckoff Avenue station off the L train. It's as if he hasn't seen me in years, the way he hugs me and lifts me off my feet. We walk through my old hood, hand in hand, talking small talk about school, college, SATs, and Bushwick. I can spot the renovations happening to our old building from a block away.

The windows have been taken out, and the whole inside of the building has been gutted. My stomach sinks, and a wave of sadness makes me want to fall to the ground and wail. Darius squeezes my hand.

"Do you know who bought it?" I ask.

"Does it matter?" he says.

"Yeah, you might not like your new neighbors." I smile.

"You're right. There'll probably be some rich white girl who'll be afraid of me and then she'll realize that I'm not that bad since I go to private school and all and we'll fall madly in love and the rest is history."

"Why you trying to put that out there like that, Darius?"

"Are you jealous?"

"Hell yeah!" I say.

"Well, don't be, 'cause I want to show you something."

We get closer to my old building, and I notice that the crumbling sidewalk has been repaved. A tree stump that used to be there is now gone, and so is the rickety gate. My heart feels like it's about to split in half. In about a year, I won't recognize this place.

Darius pulls my hand and crouches down on the ground right in front of the building. And I immediately start laughing. "What are you doing?" I ask. It's the corniest and sweetest thing I've ever seen. In elementary school, we'd spray paint on the handball wall, or on a park bench. But since sidewalks don't usually get paved in this part of the hood, initials carved into the concrete are something I don't usually see.

"I wish I could've showed off my artistic skills a little better," Darius says with a huge smile on his face. "But I know you want me to . . . K.I.S.S."

"Boy, I am not crouching down on that ground to kiss you!" I say, laughing.

"No. I just kept it simple stupid. K, I, S, S." He grins from ear to ear, as if he just said the cleverest thing.

"You know what? With all that fancy education, you sure know how to keep it original."

"I try," he says. "So. Do you like?"

Right there, in front of the place I used to call home, the place I spent the first seventeen years of my life, are the letters and words Z + D FOREVER inside a heart with an arrow.

"I love it," I say, taking his hand as he gets up from the ground. "So, forever?"

"Forever," he says, slipping his arms around my waist. "Well . . . that will be there forever if they don't repave it." He tries to hold in a laugh.

I punch him lightly on the arm and say, "You *wish* it could be there forever, Darius Darcy!"

I wrap my arms around his shoulders, pull him in, and give Darius a deep, long kiss for what feels like forever.

ACKNOWLEDGMENTS

I wanted to write a love story filled with sweetness, joy, and beauty. But our current political situation was a constant noise and distraction. So much was happening in the world, and at times, it was hard to focus on the magic of first love. The early drafts of something almost like a love story were a muddy pool of disappointment, anger, and fear. I needed an anchor—a structure to hold on to, something that would guide this love story toward healing and reconciliation, if not for the characters themselves, then for me.

Thank you to the great literary figure Jane Austen, for writing and publishing *Pride and Prejudice* in 1813, amidst everything that was happening in her world at the time. Austen gifted us with a story about not only love but class, expectations, and a woman's place in the world. Even as she, a woman in nineteenth-century England, had the audacity to write, observe, and speak truth to power with such wit, humor, and grace.

Thank you to my dear husband of eighteen years, Joseph. The memories we share allowed me to tap into sweetness, tenderness, and of course, revolution.

Thank you to my many high school secret crushes, soulmates, this-is-forevers, one-and-only-trues, unrequited loves, hate-love-hate-agains, and infatuations. I have enough love stories to last me a lifetime.

I am ever grateful to my teen daughters, Abadai and Bahati, wise, opinionated, no-holds-barred beta readers; as well as my son, Zuberi, who couldn't care less, but I have to include him.

Ammi-Joan Paquette, thank you for always championing my ideas and visions. I am truly honored to have you as a literary agent, and to be a part of the wonderful EMLA.

I could not have tackled a *Pride and Prejudice* retelling without my editor extraordinaire and super Austen fan, Alessandra Balzer. Thank you so much for loving these characters and rooting for them.

Thank you to Team Zuri at Alloy. Hayley Wagreich, your attention to detail is truly one for the books. Literally. I've learned so much from you. Thank you, Sara Shandler, for your unwavering enthusiasm. Josh Bank, Joelle Hobeika, and Les Morgenstein, thank you for crossing uncharted roads and paving new paths. It has been a wonderful journey.

I'm so proud and honored to be a part of the Balzer + Bray/ HarperCollins family. Thank you, Kelsey Murphy, Donna Bray, Kate Jackson, Suzanne Murphy, Andrea Pappenheimer, Kerry Moynagh, Kathy Faber, Jen Wygand, Jessica Malone, Megan Beatie, Olivia Russo, Patty Rosati, Molly Motch, Nellie Kurtzman, Ebony LaDelle, Bess Braswell, Alison Donalty, Mark Rifkin, Renée Cafiero, Caitlin Garing, Kristen Eckhardt, and Vanessa Nuttry—you've all made my dreams come true.

I could not have asked for a better voice for Zuri than Elizabeth Acevedo—a wise and passionate wordsmith. Thank you so much for your friendship and lending your dope performance skills to this story.

I'm immensely grateful to Jacqueline Woodson, whose books *Brown Girl Dreaming* and *Another Brooklyn* capture our shared first neighborhood of Bushwick with such care and love.

Finally, I can't even put into words how excited I am about the brilliant work of art that is the cover! A giant hug to designer Jenna Stempel-Lobell for bringing together two incredible artists, Bill Ellis and T. S. Abe. From the bottom of my heart, thank you! You've beautifully captured these two kids in a place that's chipped at the center, broken at the edges, and held together by love.

Thank you, Bushwick and Brooklyn, for the memories of home and that ever-pervasive New York hustle.

IBI ZOBOI

is the author of *American Street*, a National Book Award finalist. She was born in Port-au-Prince, Haiti, and holds an MFA in writing for children and young adults from Vermont College of Fine Arts. Her writing has been published in the *New York Times Book Review*, *The Horn Book*, and the Rumpus, among others. She lives in Brooklyn with her husband and their three children.

You can find her online at www.ibizoboi.net.

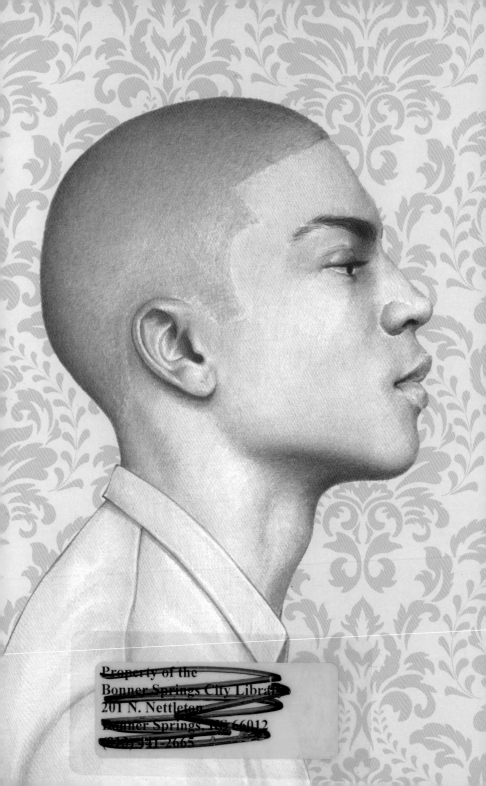